PUFFIN BOOKS

The Ramayana

The Ramayana

Adapted by Pratima Mitchell

PUFFIN BOOKS

Dedicated to the memory of my father, Prem Bhatia

With thanks to Professor Tapan Raychaudhri

PUFFIN BOOKS

Published by the Penguin Group
Penguin Books Ltd, 27 Wrights Lane, London w8 5tz, England
Penguin Books USA Inc., 375 Hudson Street, New York, New York 10014, USA
Penguin Books Australia Ltd, Ringwood, Victoria, Australia
Penguin Books Canada Ltd, 10 Alcorn Avenue, Toronto, Ontario, Canada m4v 3b2
Penguin Books (NZ) Ltd, 182–190 Wairau Road, Auckland 10, New Zealand

Penguin Books Ltd, Registered Offices: Harmondsworth, Middlesex, England

Puffin Film and TV Tie-in edition first published 1996
1 3 5 7 9 10 8 6 4 2

Filmset in 13/16pt Monophoto Palatino by
Datix International Limited, Bungay, Suffolk

Made and printed in England by Clays Ltd, St Ives plc

Contents

Introduction

*T*hroughout the whole Indian subcontinent, children look forward to the great annual festivals of Dasehra and Diwali. Dasehra comes first in October, when the story of Prince Rama is acted in the open air for the community to enjoy. Once the paper figure of arch-demon Ravan has been destroyed in a huge bonfire, and Good has triumphed visibly and publicly over Evil, then the return of Rama and Sita from exile is celebrated by Diwali, the festival of lights.

All Hindu children in India know the story of Rama. In villages and towns parents, grandparents, aunts and uncles pass on the many exciting and moving tales of the *Ramayana* to younger family members. The adventures and trials of Rama, Sita,

Lakshman and Hanuman the monkey god have been part of people's imagination for many thousands of years, and different regions have their own versions of the stories. Beginning with stories that were recited and sung orally, the many versions of the *Ramayana* were written down by poets over the centuries. The three best-known and most beautiful versions were composed by Valmiki, Tulsidas and Kamban.

Recently, the *Ramayana* was made into a television series. It was shown every Sunday for over a year. All over India, children and adults would let nothing and nobody interfere with their viewing each week. Whoever owned a television set in a village or neighbourhood allowed their friends, relatives and acquaintances to come and catch up with the latest episode. Like Dasehra, the televising of the *Ramayana* became a focal point for families, friends, neighbourhoods and communities to enjoy together.

The re-enactment of the *Ramayana* over the Dasehra period is called Ramlila. Usually it takes place over three days, but it can last a whole month. In the town of Benares (or Varanasi), which is specially sacred for the Hindus, the *Ramayana* is performed over thirty-one days, the entire town and surrounding countryside being used as settings for the story. The Maharaja of Benares himself plays a key role in the drama and helps to finance the project year after year.

The roles of Rama, Sita, Lakshman, Bharat, Shatrughan and the monkeys are played by young boys aged about twelve or thirteen. Being chosen to act is a great honour; during the period of preparation and throughout the performance the young actors are treated with great respect by everyone — the boys who play Rama, Sita, Lakshman and Hanuman are almost worshipped as divine beings by the thousands of people who come to watch day after day.

Although Rama is the perfect man and Sita the perfect woman for Hindus, Rama is much more than a superhero. He is worshipped as another form of the god Vishnu. Hindus believe that Rama was a god born as a man, as was Krishna. Rama and Krishna are the two best-loved gods in the Hindu religion.

Episodes in the story are taken as examples of how one should behave, and the conduct of Rama and Sita in particular is seen as a model for ordinary human actions. Rama's love and respect for his father, Sita's faithfulness and kindness, Lakshman and Bharat's warm, brotherly feelings and Hanuman's courage and friendship are admired by all. In dark contrast to their shining virtues are Kaikeyi's selfishness and the demons' greed and cruelty. Even the relationship between the monkey brothers, Bali and Sugriv is compared indirectly with Rama, Lakshman, Bharat and Shatrughan's loyalty to one another.

Rama's name is sacred to Hindus and is often chanted as a simple prayer early in the morning. Instead of 'Hello, how are you?' many Indians will greet one another with 'Rama, Rama!' The words used in the marriage ceremony of Rama and Sita are still used in weddings today. At funerals, the name of Rama is chanted by the pallbearers: 'The name of Rama is Truth.' When the leader of the Indian Independence movement, Mahatma Gandhi, was murdered by a fellow Hindu, his last words were, 'Rama, Rama!'

During Ramlila at Dasehra, spectators cheer Rama and Lakshman's victories and boo the entrances and exits of the baddies. After the great battle scene between Rama and Ravan, enormous paper figures of Ravan and his brother, Kumbhkarna are triumphantly set on fire. Fireworks light up the night sky and all the onlookers sweeten their mouths with sticky sweets. It reminds people that Good *will* win over Evil and that it is important to know right from wrong.

Soon afterwards comes the enchanting festival of Diwali, the festival of lights. Every Hindu home in India is decorated with tiny earthenware lamps, brimming with oil and lit with cotton wicks. Diwali night is a magical sight, and once again fireworks fizz and bang and throw explosions of coloured stars against the velvety dark sky. Rama, Sita and Lakshman have now returned home after their fourteen years of exile from Ayodhya. Ravan has been sent off to the under-world, and peace and goodwill will now reign for many years under good King Rama. *Ramrajya*, meaning in the time of Rama, is the ideal state of harmony between a ruler and his subjects when good government, justice and peace are the order of the day. Even now in India, politicians promise to bring about *Ramrajya* and contentment if only people will vote for them.

And it is not only Hindus in India who keep alive the tradition of the *Ramayana*, but also many countries of South-East Asia — Java and Sumatra in Indonesia, Malaysia, Cambodia and Burma — have had large Hindu communities from very early times. They too remember the story of Rama and Sita through their dance, drama, painting and beautiful crafts. Non-Hindus enjoy the drama and excitement of Rama's and Sita's adventures.

Like all epics, the *Ramayana* is to do with heroism, suffering and sacrifice on a grand scale. But it is unique among epics in being relevant to millions of Hindus, of all classes and backgrounds, who turn to it for inspiration and comfort in their daily lives.

1 How Rama was Born

Years ago, when the world was young, the gods met together to discuss their concerns. Evil had started to affect people's lives. Now suspicion and fear – never part of the gods' plans for their creation – were becoming commonplace. Peace and harmony, which had been taken for granted, just like air and water, had been snatched away by rakshasas, or demons, who had become powerful.

Many good and wise kings and queens ruled over prosperous kingdoms, but it was becoming more and more difficult for them to protect all their subjects, especially those who lived in remote places, far from cities. It was these innocent people who were being troubled the most by rakshasas and evil creatures, chief among whom was Ravan, King of Lanka.

Ravan was as mighty and powerful as any of the gods. He owned vaults full of precious jewels and gold, he was master of many fortified cities and commanded armies of countless demons. He was tremendously conceited about his amazing supernatural and magical powers. No one had ever defeated him in war, and he rejoiced in being the arch-enemy of everything good.

Physically he towered over men, as he was enormously tall. With his ten heads, twenty copper-coloured eyes and twenty arms, he was a fearsome sight. Day and night his demon battalions were busy creating the most wicked tactics with which they disturbed the peace of the world. The prayers of saints and hermits, rising like incense to protect and purify the atmosphere, were constantly interrupted by evil beings. Young women never knew when they might be kidnapped by Ravan's minions to add to their master's collection of slaves. The whole order of the universe was threatened by Ravan's evil. Ravan was safe from the anger of the gods because Brahma, whom Hindus regard as God the Creator, had (for some purpose of his own) granted Ravan special protection; however, although he was safe from attack by heavenly beings, Brahma had not given him protection from men.

When the gods reminded Brahma of their helplessness against Ravan, he told them not to despair. In his grand design to preserve the supremacy of Good over Evil, the god Vishnu was going to be born as a man. This superhuman man would defeat Ravan in a great battle and establish a time of peace and prosperity for the human race.

So when the gods cried out to Brahma, 'Is there such a hero who, among all the heroes in this world, has every quality of virtue, wisdom and strength?', the answer came back, 'Yes. There is Rama, the son of King Dasharath of the Ikshvaku dynasty, descended from the Sun itself.'

In Hindu belief, Rama is the perfect man, a man who conquered evil by defeating Ravan and who is worshipped as a god, since he originated from Vishnu himself. And this is how he was brought into the world.

King Dasharath was the best of kings. He ruled over the land of Koshal with kindness and wisdom. His capital, Ayodhya, was a moated city with bright, beautiful buildings and artistically laid-out parks. His people were happy and contented since Dasharath understood their needs and treated them fairly. They had to pay very few taxes and were fortunate because their king had clever advisers, holy priests and scholars to help him with planning and decisions.

Dasharath was very happy with his three wives, but he longed to make his happiness complete by having children. None of his wives had given him a child. Since he was growing old, he decided to try to please the gods one last time by performing a great sacrifice. He thought that if the gods heeded his yearning and heard the ardent prayers of his wives, then perhaps they would give him the gift of a child.

After consulting his priests, King Dasharath let loose a splendid white horse into the countryside. The animal roamed around freely for a year, and at the end of that time it was brought back to the palace and sacrificed. An enormous pit in the shape of an eagle was dug in the ground, incense and sweet-smelling firewood were burnt in it and prayers recited. The logs crackled, spitting golden stars into the air. The flames roared and thick smoke hung in a cloud over the king and his priests.

Suddenly the flames increased and shot up to the sky, and from the trembling haze of heat and light a shining figure appeared. 'Your prayers will be answered,' said the messenger of the gods, addressing the king. 'Here is a golden bowl of sweet milk pudding from the gods. Give some to your wives and you will be blessed with sons.' The figure then dissolved back into the fire.

The king first prayed then fed his three wives the

rice pudding, and very soon afterwards they became pregnant. Kausalya, the eldest, was the first to give birth. Her son was Rama. Then Sumitra, the middle wife, gave birth to twins, Lakshman and Shatrughan. Kaikeyi, the youngest and most beautiful queen, gave birth to Bharat.

And this, Hindus believe, is the story of how Rama was born to represent the Almighty and to fulfil his destiny as an example to the whole of mankind.

2 The First Test

The four princes, Rama, Lakshman, Shatrughan and Bharat, grew up together as great friends. But Rama's closest companion was Lakshman. Rama was tall and handsome, with an athlete's build. He never lost his temper and was patient and kind towards everyone. He always spoke the truth, but without hurting others' feelings. He was fearless, brave and adventurous; above all his other virtues, Rama honoured and respected his father and his three wives, all of whom he called Mother.

Lakshman was like Rama's shadow. The younger brother hero-worshipped Rama but, unlike his older brother, he had a fiery temper. If he saw an act of injustice or unfairness, he would speak out, strum impatiently on his bowstring and scowl fiercely. Sometimes Rama had to calm him down.

All four brothers were educated by the best teachers. They learned Sanskrit and the scriptures, archery, swordsmanship and correct behaviour. As they grew into young men, they were adored by the people of Koshal, who prayed for the safety and happiness of their royal family and thanked the gods for giving them such noble princes.

When Rama was almost sixteen, his father began to think about finding a princess for his eldest son. In those days it was usual for boys to get married at such a young age. Before King Dasharath could despatch his courtiers to learn where suitable princesses might be found, something unexpected happened.

Dasharath was discussing state matters with his chief adviser, a holy sage named Vashishta, when the loud, lowing call of conch shells from the palace gates announced a visitor. The courtiers bowed deeply with folded hands to pay respect to a white-haired hermit who was entering the hall. He was a sage even more famous and holy than Vashishta, and his name was Vishwamitra. Wearing a deerskin and carrying a wooden staff, his long hair matted with the milky liquid of the banyan tree, Vishwamitra strode up to the throne. Without making any of the usual polite enquiries he said abruptly to the king, 'I have come to ask you a favour.' Dasharath felt very honoured. Vishwamitra continued, 'I am in the middle of special prayers and sacrifices to the gods in my forest hermitage, but the foul demons Mareech and Subahu keep disturbing me. They torment me while I am praying so that I cannot concentrate. My spells are not working against them and I need your son Rama to come with me to destroy these monsters.'

At first Dasharath was shocked into silence. After a few moments he said, 'Rama is still too young and untried. He has no experience of fighting wily devils like Mareech and Subahu.'

Vishwamitra looked annoyed. He was a person whom even the gods were afraid to cross and, even though he was a powerful king, Dasharath was only a man. Very reluctantly the king agreed to let his eldest son accompany the great sage, but on the condition that Lakshman went as well.

'Fear not for the safety of your sons, O King,' Vishwamitra promised. 'They will be protected and they will return to you stronger and wiser in every way.'

The two princes slung their bows over their shoulders, said goodbye to their parents and younger brothers, and followed Vishwamitra across the River Sarayu, which separated Ayodhya from the largely uninhabited wilderness beyond. After walking for a whole day, they crossed the River Ganga (the holiest of all rivers), where Vishwamitra taught them two secret spells which would keep them from feeling tired and would protect them from harm. Rama and Lakshman showed their respect for the holy river by bowing to it, then they all continued their journey which would bring them to the Dandak forest.

Vishwamitra's home was deep in the forest. He lived, along with other holy men, in a place of prayer and worship known as an ashram. It was in a remote, dark spot where the trees seemed to reach the sky and forbid the entry of even a single ray of sunshine. Using their swords like scythes, Rama and Lakshman hacked their way through creepers and thickets. In between the swish-swish sound of their swords they could hear the roar of lions and tigers. Boars rampaged in the undergrowth and wild elephants crashed through the bamboo. Never before had they been in such an eerie place. Vishwamitra pointed in a northerly direction. 'Your first task is to kill the mother of Mareech. Her name is Tataka and she lives in that cave over there.'

Rama immediately strung his bow and played on the string as a warning. The humming sound spiralled through the air and vibrated loudly in Tataka's ear. 'Who dares to disturb me?' she shrieked, bounding through the forest towards the three men. She was a hideously ugly ogress, her face was distorted with rage, her eyes were the colour of blood and her slavering mouth dripped with entrails.

Rama aimed an arrow at her chest. Whistling along its curved trajectory, it struck its mark, puncturing her massive chest. A bloodcurdling scream ripped through the air as the ogress somersaulted backwards and hit the ground. She writhed and dug her long fingernails into the ground, tearing up clumps of grass and bushes and creating a great commotion. But then her roars began to subside and her huge body became still. At last she lay motionless, with her enormous, bloody mouth open in a dreadful snarl — and so ended the life of the mother of Mareech.

Rama's first victory over the forces of evil led to great celebrations in heaven. The gods, who were very friendly with Vishwamitra, signalled that he should continue to teach Rama and Lakshman the secrets which only they knew.

Vishwamitra was very happy to show his pleasure at Rama's performance. He took out all the divine weapons in his possession. He gave Rama and Laksh-man several deadly instruments and weapons to fight against disasters like drought, flood and sickness; then he taught them the secret spells which would activate all the weapons. He warned the brothers, 'You will need every skill and knowledge to deal with what lies ahead.'

The three pressed on until they came to Vishwamitra's ashram. The rishis who lived with him and who were his disciples prepared food and made them beds of grass. For the next six days and six nights Rama and Lakshman kept watch while Vishwamitra prayed and meditated. On the seventh day, at the end of his period of fasting and prayer, the sky around the hermitage seemed to shrivel into darkness. A terrible roaring in the forest region announced the arrival of the terrifying creatures, Mareech and Subahu.

They hovered over the ashram like black storm-clouds, furiously shaking the trees and creating cyclones which moaned and howled like demented devils. Then the monsters rained a shower of blood and rotting flesh on the holy fires which were burning outside the huts.

Choosing his moment, Rama took careful aim and flung a magic discus at Mareech. It gathered speed as it spun like a planet in orbit, then hit the monster like a thunderbolt. Lifting him up, it carried him in a flash of dark lightning hundreds of miles away to the ocean. He hit the water with a huge splash. Lakshman aimed another discus at Subahu, and this carried him off in the opposite direction. And with that the demons' reign of terror in the Dandaka forest came to an end.

Vishwamitra congratulated the brothers. 'You have completed your task and made my ashram safe once more.' He turned to Rama. 'Now it is my turn to do something for you. The next part of our journey is going to take us to the city of Mithila, where King Janak will be very happy to meet you. Ahead lies another, more pleasant task which must be fulfilled.' Then Vishwamitra and his rishis, accompanied by the two princes, started off on the second part of their journey.

3 Rama and Sita and the Coronation

Just as Rama was a special gift from the gods to Dasharath and his eldest wife Kausalya, so was Sita the gift of the earth goddess to King Janak of Mithila.

Once, when he was ploughing the ground in preparation for a great sacrifice to the gods, Janak saw a tiny baby girl lying cradled in the furrows. He and his queen named her Sita, and she grew up to become a young woman of exceptional beauty and goodness. In her face and form Janak and his wife could see all the lovely, fresh qualities of Nature. Just as a beautiful landscape inspires happy thoughts, so Sita inspired all who saw her.

Like Rama, Sita was of an age when her parents were thinking about finding the ideal marriage partner for her. Janak loved her so dearly that he was willing to give her hand only to the most exceptional man in the world. Sita's future husband would have to be valorous, valiant and virtuous. Janak wanted a hero far above ordinary heroes for his beloved daughter. To gain her hand, he decided that prospective suitors would have to prove themselves.

Years before, the wind god Varun had given him a gift, a golden bow which belonged to the god Shiva. It was so gigantic that it could be carried only by an eight-wheeled chariot. To lift and draw this bow would be the supreme challenge for any man who sought Sita's hand.

As Rama, Lakshman, Vishwamitra and his followers entered the city of Mithila, they were seen by Sita from her palace balcony. She observed the ancient sage at the head of the procession, with his wooden staff and hermit's bowl, and the two young men walking behind him. They were going in the direction of King Janak's audience chamber. Sita's eyes followed Rama as he went to meet her father. The young man walked with confidence, yet seemed modest. He looked strong, manly and dignified. Sita immediately fell in love with the handsome young prince. She wondered whether he had come to join the procession of princes, eager to bend the golden bow and win her for their bride. She hoped fervently that Rama would be the successful one.

King Janak gave the visitors a royal welcome. He was a friend of King Dasharath and he formed a favourable impression of Rama. The golden bow of Shiva was ceremoniously wheeled out, and Rama was invited to try his strength. The crowds that had gathered shut their eyes tight because they couldn't bear the tension and so they missed the exciting moment when Rama stepped forward and lifted the mighty bow effortlessly. He didn't need an arrow but, as he drew the bowstring all the way back to his right ear in a perfect V, the bow snapped as easily as a dry twig. Immediately the gods clapped their hands in applause, which to the onlookers below sounded like great peals of thunder. Everyone showered Rama with petals of rose and jasmine, so it looked as though the gods themselves had rained down the scented flowers.

The wedding of Rama and Sita was like a carnival, a festival and a sacred day in one. King Dasharath and his three wives came from Ayodhya to attend the celebrations. The men, women and children of Mithila dressed up in gossamer silks and jewellery. All the animals, from horses to elephants and cows, were washed and adorned with coloured paint, plumes and tassels. Fountains sprayed perfumed water into the air, music played on every street corner and peacocks displayed their blue-green tail-feathers. Doves cooed and mynah birds warbled. Trees came into blossom and all Nature sang together in harmony to honour the royal couple. Jasmine and hibiscus flowers were strewn on footpaths and the people of Mithila danced and sang all day and all night.

For Hindus, Rama is the ideal man and Sita the ideal woman. Hindus believe they had previously been married in heaven, and their union on earth was a continuation of their eternal love for one another.

When King Janak gave away his daughter, he told Rama she would always be faithful and stay by his side. Sita followed her prince seven times round the sacred fire as priests chanted holy scriptures. The chief priest married them with a blessing and special prayer which is still part of the marriage ceremony in many parts of India.

Then came a year of great happiness for Rama and Sita. In Ayodhya, Dasharath continued to rule his people with kindness and wisdom; everyone prospered, enjoying the feeling that they were living in an earthly paradise. But one morning, when Dasharath looked at himself in the mirror, he noticed that around his eyes were nests of wrinkles; deep lines scored his face and his hair had become snowy white. Age had overtaken him like a silent thief. He realized he was now an old man. That same morning, while he was signing state papers, he noticed with a start that his writing looked feebler than before. His energy and vigour were beginning to leave him for good. 'The time has come for my retirement,' he thought.

In ancient India, when the end of his active life arrived, a man was supposed to spend his time in quiet thought and meditation; Dasharath felt that he had reached this stage. He felt that now was the moment to hand over his kingly duties to someone younger.

With these thoughts in mind, he called his old friend and adviser, the sage Vashishta. 'I think you and all the people of Ayodhya will agree that Rama is totally trustworthy, totally honourable and totally just. He is courageous and loving, and he makes no distinction between the high-born and the low-born. He is an affectionate son, husband, brother and friend, and is devoted to preserving righteousness in all areas of life. In short, do you not agree that he will be the ideal king? I have made up my mind to appoint him my successor and I don't want any delay in the proceedings. Let us begin preparations for the ceremony immediately,' he concluded.

Rama was sent for and Dasharath told him that he had decided to make the young prince his successor to the throne. Rama folded his hands in front of him and bowed in submission to his father's wishes.

That night Dasharath had dreadful nightmares. In the morning he consulted his wise men, who told him that the times were not auspicious; they added that it was possible that a tragedy was about to take place in his life. His heart beat uncomfortably fast and he was overwhelmed by a sense of doom. He sent for Rama again and said, 'I have an uneasy feeling that something terrible is about to happen – last night I may have seen the herald of my own death. For that reason I am going to bring forward the date of your coronation. It will now be held tomorrow. You and Sita must hurry and start preparing for the ceremonies by fasting and prayer. Go and begin what you have to do, and Vashishta will assist you.'

Rama went to his own apartments in the royal palace to tell Sita about the plans which were to bring new responsibilities and change their lives for ever.

4 A Reversal of Plans

While Dasharath had been talking to his eldest son, the news of his important decision somehow spread outside the private chambers. A courtier might have whispered a few words of gossip to a doorman who, in turn, passed them on to a serving maid, who spoke to the cook, who then informed the washerman. Whichever way it was conveyed, by dusk almost the whole of Ayodhya knew that Rama was to be crowned their sovereign the next day.

Rama was greatly loved by the people, so in no time at all they started to plan the festivities which would celebrate the happy event. Lamps burned all night long as men, women and children, old and young, prepared for the joyous day. Sweetmeat sellers stirred huge cauldrons of sweetened milk, while their helpers pounded almonds and sorted out mounds of dried grapes and dates. Flower sellers sat up all night stringing wreaths of waxy white jasmine flowers which filled the lanes with their heady perfume. Mothers hastily brought out their family's best clothes, sewing on pearls and sequins to make them look even more splendid. Musicians tuned their instruments to welcome in the dawn. Small boys climbed up tamarind trees to loop coloured bunting through the branches and to reserve good seats for the next day's courtly procession. In the palace precincts, the keepers of the royal animals bathed the elephants and groomed the horses for the parade. Children couldn't sleep for excitement and their happy chatter arose in the normally tranquil night air.

In the palace of Dasharath's youngest queen, Kaikeyi, a woman-in-waiting called Manthara went out on to the balcony for a breath of air. Stars were just starting to prick the evening sky and a new moon had scratched a pinstripe curve in the distance. Idly she gazed at the city down below and she was startled at what she saw: lights blazing, people thronging the streets, activity of a kind she had never known before. Hymns of praise floated up to where she stood, watching, and the laughter of children reached her ears.

'Whatever is going on?' she muttered to herself. She hobbled downstairs as fast as she was able (being very ungainly and awkward, due to a hump on her back), to ask the palace guards what was going on.

'Don't you know? You are the one who always hears the news before anybody else: you, with eyes at the back of your head and your ears forever close to the ground!' they teased. 'How could you have missed the wonderful news of Rama's coronation tomorrow?' they added, pleased for once that they had an advantage over her, for Manthara made no secret of her influence over Queen Kaikeyi to the other servants.

Like a tortoise hunched inside its shell, Manthara narrowed her eyes and brooded over the news she had just received. The more she thought, the more fantasies chased around in her imagination.

Why had Dasharath suddenly decided to crown Rama as his successor?

Had he deliberately timed his announcement to coincide with Kaikeyi's son Bharat's visit to his grandfather?

Was Dasharath planning to banish Bharat and exile Kaikeyi? If that happened, what would she, Manthara, do? Where would she go in her old age?

After all, Kaikeyi was known to be his favourite

wife. Why was he not rewarding the son of her womb in the manner in which he deserved? Besides, why had Dasharath not come in person to tell Kaikeyi about his plans? Obviously this was meant to be an insult to her beautiful young mistress.

Manthara worked herself up into such a state that she went storming into Kaikeyi's chamber. 'Get up, get up, this is no time to lie around getting your legs massaged. The world is crashing round your ears, and all you do is indulge yourself! Catastrophe awaits you, O mother of Bharat! Open your ears and your eyes. Protect yourself and your son!'

Kaikeyi turned lazily around on her side and signalled to her serving-women to pause in their beauty treatments. 'Manthara, Manthara,' she said tolerantly. She was very fond of her maid, who had accompanied her from her father's palace when she had come as King Dasharath's young bride. 'What are you ranting about?'

'Ranting? I, ranting? You had better think about what you say, mistress, or you'll soon be without a roof over your head!' the waiting-woman exclaimed, recklessly embroidering her fantasy even further.

Kaikeyi sat up abruptly, a serious expression now on her face. 'Explain yourself!' she snapped. 'Whatever do you mean? What is this nonsense talk?'

'All over Ayodhya the people are getting ready for

Rama's coronation tomorrow!' Manthara paused, looking hard at Kaikeyi. 'And you, whom he calls "Mother", doesn't know anything about it,' Manthara continued, happy that she had at last managed to rattle her mistress.

'What are you saying?' Kaikeyi demanded.

'Your husband,' the old woman managed to make the word sound like an injury, 'is abdicating the throne tomorrow. Rama is being crowned king; and there's no coincidence in the fact that Bharat is far away at this time, visiting your father. Now listen to me, my child —' her voice dropped '— listen to your old nurse: Dasharath must not be allowed to indulge in such foolishness. He owes you a favour, remember, from the time you saved his life after he had been terribly wounded in a battle. He promised you then that whatever you should ever want would be yours. Ask him now to give Bharat the throne and banish Rama to the forest! He must be gone for a long time — fourteen years — by which time Bharat will have established himself in the hearts of the people.'

Kaikeyi shook her head so that her long black hair waved like a silken curtain. She laughed, showing her small, pearly teeth. 'Oh, Manthara, you are a silly old woman. Why should it worry me if Rama becomes king? He is just like a son to me, and he will make an excellent king to succeed my husband. Now, now, go and find something better to do with your mischievous mind. I know, look out my clothes for tomorrow's coronation. I want to look my best for my dear Rama.'

Manthara stamped her foot. She was allowed to take such liberties with her mistress, having looked after her since she was a toddler. 'Foolish, foolish queen,' she chided, 'and, who knows, queen for how much longer? Here is an opportunity sent by Fate, but you seem blind to your own interests. I entreat you, my dear, listen to me.'

Now at this point something happened in Kaikeyi's heart. As though a serpent had injected its poisonous venom into her normally loving and generous nature, her mind started to fill with unworthy thoughts. Once she allowed in one wrong idea, several more followed rapidly. She bit her lip and clasped her hands with tension.

Manthara relaxed; she knew that she had won. 'This is what you have to do, my child: when the king visits you this evening, let him find you in a state of deep unhappiness. Do not speak to him or answer any questions until he begs you to ask for whatever you wish. Then, strike like a cobra attacking its victim and allow him no mercy until you have his promise: to enthrone Bharat and banish Rama to the forest for fourteen years.'

Kaikeyi chewed her nails, walking restlessly up and down her chamber. Abruptly she gave an order for the oil lamps to be dimmed; she flung off her silken gown, tore off her pearls and squeezed her golden bracelets off her wrists. She tossed her long hair this way and that until it resembled a haystack, and then she worked herself up into a state of hysteria.

And this is how King Dasharath found her when he came to tell her the happy news of Rama's coronation. Instead of a lovely, smiling face, Dasharath saw a sulky, dishevelled wife whose lotus-like cheeks were stained with tears.

'My dear, what is it?' he said tenderly, fearfully distressed that someone had offended his favourite wife. 'Tell me who the culprit is,' he said, continuing to misread the situation, 'and I will punish him or her.'

Kaikeyi refused to talk to him, just as she had been coached by Manthara. Finally, when she had her lord and master on bended knees, begging her to explain the cause of her dark mood, she said, 'Do you remember the time when I nursed you back to life after a great battle? And you promised me two wishes? Well, the time has come to fulfil your pledge. I want you to grant me two wishes.'

The king was so relieved to have extracted a few words from her that he immediately gave his solemn oath that she would have whatever she wished.

Kaikeyi rose from the floor where she had been lying sprawled like a wounded heron, held out her hand and said, 'I want you to crown my son Bharat king of Ayodhya instead of Rama. And my second wish is that Rama be banished to the forest for fourteen years.'

5 The Exile

Kaikeyi was determined to get her own way, even though her aged husband was grieved beyond measure by her demands. Her kind heart had become transformed into an unforgiving one and her once beautiful face into a stony mask.

All Dasharath's pleading and entreaties made not the slightest impact. 'But you love Rama as a son,' he appealed to her. 'He is the eldest. The people worship him and want him as their king.'

Kaikeyi started to comb her hair, an expression of disdain on her face.

Dasharath tried another argument. 'I have already told Rama that he is to be crowned king in the morning. How can I take back my word?'

'And you can take back the word you gave me?' she snapped. 'Is your promise to me so worthless that men in future times will talk of you as the mighty ruler whose word was never to be trusted?'

'And I, how will I live without my beloved Rama? Do you not care about my feelings? Is this to be my end in old age, at the time when I should put aside cares and worries? Am I to die of grief and a broken heart?' he pleaded.

Kaikeyi's supreme lack of concern made him realize that she would never change her mind.

'You are a base and wicked creature. A she-devil whom the whole world will remember as the destroyer of my family.' He turned away from her in disgust. 'You are my wife no longer. From today you are a stranger to me!'

'Come, come,' said Kaikeyi. 'Send for your darling son and tell him the news. The coronation ceremonies must be postponed until Bharat returns from my father's house. Don't stand around, wringing your hands like a helpless old woman; there is much to be done this night.'

But the night was now fading into dawn and the new day, the day of Rama's coronation, had arrived. With the taste of ashes and bile in his mouth, King Dasharath knew that things could never again be the same. From the open window of Kaikeyi's chambers he heard the ringing of temple bells and morning hymns being sung in praise of his eldest son. Birds were excitedly chirping, flowers were unfurling their petals. He heard the increasing bustle of the city waking up to the prospect of the many pleasures and celebrations which lay ahead. Alas, little did people realize that the day of gladness was going to become a day of mourning.

Like a person who has already said goodbye to the land of the living, Dasharath sent for Rama. The prince had spent the night in prayer and, along with Sita, was getting ready for the ceremonies later that morning. He and Sita had bathed and purified themselves. Vashishta had already anointed their foreheads with fresh, fragrant sandalwood paste. Dressed in fine but simple silk robes, Rama and Sita entered Kaikeyi's rooms, completely unaware of the drama that had been unfolding all night long.

Rama touched his father's feet and then moved to touch Kaikeyi's feet, but she quickly moved away from him. He looked with astonishment to his father, whom he now noticed was pale and drawn as though he was suffering from a terrible illness.

'My son,' Dasharath began in a trembling voice.

'Tell him and get it over with,' Kaikeyi prompted in her new, harsh tone.

Dasharath, however, was quite unable to speak; no

41

words came out of his mouth and he was unable to move. Without further ado, Kaikeyi immediately took control of the situation and informed Rama that the plans for the day had been altered. She told him about the promise which Dasharath had made to her and she asked if Rama would agree to help his father carry out his pledge.

'Whatever Father has agreed must be honoured,' Rama said quietly.

Kaikeyi continued, 'Your father has promised the throne to Bharat. I'm sorry to say he has banished you to the Dandak forest for a period of fourteen years.' She looked for a sign of grief, for a protest, for regret – but, to her surprise, Rama's face remained calm and unmoved.

'Very well, Mother, if that is what Father promised, then that is what will be done. I happily give up my claim to the throne in Bharat's favour.' Rama was living up to his reputation as a supremely virtuous and obedient young man.

A low moan came from Dasharath.

Rama consoled him. 'Father, do not have any regrets. I shall go and make arrangements to leave Ayodhya; but Bharat should be brought home so he can support the king.'

So far Queen Kaikeyi had got what she wanted; but she could not look into the future and see the consequences of her actions. She could not foretell that when Bharat found out what had taken place that morning he would despise her and never let her forget what she had done.

As soon as Lakshman heard what had happened, he lost his temper. He shook his fist, storming and railing against the injustice of the king's decree, and impetuously insisted on accompanying Rama to the forest. Sita, of course, had immediately decided that her place was by Rama's side, and she changed her coronation robes for a hermit's simple garb. Instead of silk she put on a covering made of rough tree-bark fibre. She removed most of her jewellery, keeping only a few things of sentimental value. She slipped off her golden sandals and put on a pair of wooden clogs, and she gave away her perfumes and toiletries to her maidservants. Rama and Lakshman also took off their fine things and now, also wearing rough bark-fibre clothes, they went to say goodbye to their mothers, Sumitra and Kausalya.

6 Dasharath's End and Bharat's Return

Sumantra was King Dasharath's charioteer. Serving the royal family with total devotion, he was a man full of goodness, selflessly attached to them all. Even though he was one of the king's closest advisers, he was not a man to take advantage of his privileged position.

From boyhood, the princes had been entrusted to him, and Sumantra taught them all he knew: he instructed them in the skills of handling a chariot, which could be a deadly advantage in the battlefield, and showed them how to look after the horses.

Now he waited by the palace gates, his head

bowed in sadness, reluctant but ready to carry Rama, Lakshman and Sita to the forest. As the royal chariot rolled through the gates and across the moat, the people of Ayodhya mobbed their departing princes and princess. 'Don't go, don't go,' they begged. 'Look, we have made garlands for you, composed songs about you, prepared a wonderful feast in your honour. How can you leave us when we love you so much?'

Thousands of men, women and children were following the chariot and milling round it so that Sumantra was forced to rein in the horses and make them move forward at the slowest possible pace. But still the people wept and shouted and pleaded for Rama, Sita and Lakshman not to leave.

At last Rama told Sumantra to stop the chariot so that he could speak to the crowd. 'All three of us are going into exile without any feelings of anger or bitterness. I am doing what every noble person would do, which is to honour a father's command. I am only interested in following the way of righteousness and duty, for, if a link is broken in that shining chain, evil can gain advantage. My father made a sacred promise and I am simply helping him to fulfil it. Go back to Ayodhya and follow Bharat as your king. He is a man of rare qualities and will treat each one of you with justice and kindness.' His speech only caused a fresh outbreak of protest and pleading.

A small boy ran up to the chariot and garlanded Rama with white jasmine and oleander flowers. A little girl was lifted up by her father so that she could give Sita her gift of home-made sweets. A group of singers clashed their finger-cymbals and sang a sad song of farewell to their beloved princes and princess.

Only with the greatest difficulty was Rama finally able to persuade the people to turn back home, and at last they obeyed him, but with very heavy hearts and many backward glances.

The royal entourage arrived at the banks of the sacred River Ganga. Rama and Lakshman had travelled across it once before with Vishwamitra. Now they bade goodbye to Sumantra. Rama consoled the old charioteer, who was wiping the tears from his eyes. He asked him to take loving messages to Dasharath, Kausalya and Sumitra. He even remembered to include Kaikeyi, in case she thought he had left Ayodhya in anger against her.

As Sumantra waved them goodbye, the two brothers and Sita boarded a river punt and were poled slowly across the Ganga to the far bank. Here a holy man advised them to make for the hill of Chitrakoot which, he told them, would be a peaceful and lovely retreat for their fourteen years in the forest of Dandak.

*

When he could see them no longer, Sumantra spurred on his horses to a gallop, raced his chariot back to the palace at Ayodhya and hurried indoors to convey Rama, Lakshman and Sita's messages to the old king and his wives. Outside, an atmosphere of deadly gloom hung over the city. Dusty ribbons of bunting lay trampled underfoot, all the houses and shops were shuttered and the people hid indoors, nursing their grief. The fountains had stopped playing, the lights had been extinguished and even the birds seemed to have ceased their singing.

Inside the palace, servants padded around on silent feet and spoke in whispers, because King Dasharath was lying sick on his bed and refusing to eat or speak. Very quietly Sumantra approached his bedside and gave him the news from Rama, Sita and Lakshman. 'They said you were not to worry about them. They said to tell you that they were in good spirits and that the fourteen years will pass like a dream. They sent you and the queens their love and greetings and asked that you would remember them in your prayers.'

As Sumantra finished talking, the king broke into a fresh bout of weeping. His eldest wife, Kausalya, Rama's mother, took his hands and begged him to compose himself.

'How can I be composed after what I have done

and after what I was forced to do by that she-devil? My son, my sons, my daughter-in-law! I must have done some terrible deeds in my past life to reap the fruits of my wickedness in this way.' He fell silent, thinking. 'Kausalya, my beloved queen, I know what I am paying the price for. It is now as clear as daylight. Many years ago I was hunting in the forest, following a deer which was just too sprightly for me. I tracked it to the River Sarayu, and from where I stood I thought I saw it move near the water. Taking aim, I let fly an arrow which found its target, because an anguished cry came from the riverbank. Very pleased that I had pinned down my quarry, I hurried forward to pick it up; instead of a deer, I was horrified to see that my arrow had felled a young Brahmin boy, who lay by the water, dying.

'"What have you done?" he sobbed. "I am the only son of my old, blind parents who live in the ashram near by. They are waiting for me to bring them back a pitcher of water. Now they will never see me alive again," and, as he was speaking, he died in my arms. I carried the boy's body to the parents, laid him on the ground and begged them to forgive me for the unspeakable sin I had committed. You cannot imagine how wretched I felt, or imagine their extreme anguish at realizing what had happened. When their initial grief had subsided, the old man said to me, "What has been done to us will be done to you. You too will have a son and you too will suffer a terrible loss one day." At that time we had no children and no hope of having any, and my first thought was that this was a prophecy about our future children. But it truly was a prophecy with a sting in its tail.'

After confiding in Kausalya, King Dasharath never regained his strength or his will to live, and his life slowly ebbed away.

Bharat, the heir designate, was still at his grand-father's palace, knowing nothing about the recent tragedies which had taken place at home. He, of course, had no part in Manthara and Kaikeyi's plot to place him on the throne. Now Sumantra was sent to call him back so that he could perform the funeral rites for Dasharath and take his place as ruler of Ayodhya. Vashishta, the chief adviser, warned Suman-tra not to say any more than that he was to return home immediately. So, when Bharat arrived back, he learned of his father's death, Kaikeyi's cruel demand, and Rama, Sita and Lakshman's banishment all in one heart-stopping moment.

Being completely innocent of any knowledge of his mother's manipulations, and being himself very close to Rama, Bharat was beside himself with grief and rage. He decided immediately to meet Rama in the forest, determined that he would succeed where others had failed in persuading Rama to return.

The Ramayana *is not only about the confrontation of Good and Evil, it is also about the highest and noblest aspirations of men and women, and particularly about the strength and constancy of love. Bharat's love for his brother is an example which Hindus are encouraged to aspire to.*

All the while, Rama, Sita and Lakshman were setting up house in their new environment. Sita had lived in cities all her life and was used to being looked after by servants. She had bathed in perfumed water, hennaed the delicate soles of her feet and worn the finest weaves. She had eaten the most exquisite food off golden plates and had been treated to the sound of beautiful music all day. But she was also the daughter of mother Earth, and her heart quickly responded to the rhythms of the natural world in the forest.

Everything seemed delightful to her. She saw the sunrise behind the spreading flame-of-the-forest tree and she brushed off the pollen which drifted from the yellow mimosa flowers. She picked wild pomegranates and dates and mangoes, made her cooking fire from aloe wood and camphor, and gathered waterlily buds to decorate her hair. All the birds and small animals of the forest trusted her and kept her company when she went to gather firewood.

Lakshman built a little cottage in a clearing, and he and Rama went hunting for food whenever they needed it.

It was to this quiet spot that Bharat came after a long and tiring journey from Ayodhya. He had not come alone but with a ceremonial guard of soldiers, who carried the royal flag in their vanguard. Behind them came old Vashishta and other advisers and some of the prominent citizens of Ayodhya. They watched Rama and Bharat embrace each other and sit down to talk over the events of the recent past. They watched Rama hide his face in his hands when he heard about his father's death, and they saw how Bharat pleaded with his older brother to return as king. Then they saw Rama patiently explaining his reasons for honouring Dasharath's promise, then comforting his younger brother.

Towards the end of this momentous meeting, they saw Bharat bend down and slip Rama's sandals off his feet and bring them respectfully to his forehead. Rama had refused Bharat's request, but he had agreed that Bharat should rule Ayodhya in his place: Bharat would be the regent until Rama came back from the forest, and Bharat was going to place Rama's sandals on the throne as a symbol that Rama was the real king.

Then Bharat and his retinue left Chitrakoot for Ayodhya, and Rama, Lakshman and Sita were once more on their own in the middle of the wilderness.

7 Ravan's Sister

After Bharat and the citizens of Ayodhya had left, Chitrakoot seemed a place of sad memories. Rama thought it might be better to move further into the Dandak forest. The two brothers and Sita gathered their few belongings and moved on, staying for several months at a time with different holy men, or rishis, in their ashrams. Wherever they went they were kindly received. The rishis taught them about prayer and meditation, and their wives made friends with Sita. Rama, Sita and Lakshman learned about many mysteries of the mind and spirit, and their bodies became strong and hardy.

Ten years passed and now they were inexperienced youngsters no longer but mature adults. In just three or four more years it would be time to go back to Ayodhya and time for Rama to take up his rightful position on the throne.

One of the greatest of the wise forest rishis now advised Rama to build himself a cottage in a place called Panchavati, on the banks of the River Godavari, and to complete the remainder of his exile there. Once again they packed their things and travelled on, now even further away from where they had begun their journey.

As they were on their way to Panchavati, Rama and Lakshman, always poised to fend off danger, spotted a huge bird perched at the top of a tree. Its sharp eyes seemed to follow them closely as they cleared a path through the bushes for Sita. Lakshman wondered if it was a demon in disguise, waiting to ambush them, and he strung his bow, ready for action. The eagle-like bird lifted its enormous wings and floated down in a rush of air. Sita flinched, thinking it might attack her, but the eagle opened its beak, saying in soft tones that he meant no harm and that he was their friend.

'I am Jatayu, the brother of Sampati. I was a friend of your dear father, Dasharath. The gods have given me the task of looking after Sita. Whenever you need to go hunting, I will always be close at hand and you need not worry about her safety,' he said. Jatayu followed the trio to Panchavati, hopping from treetop to treetop, keeping a lookout for any danger.

Panchavati was even more lovely than Chitrakoot, and the forest around was full of fruit trees. Again Lakshman used his building skills to construct a delightful home of wattle and daub and roofed it with palm leaves. Soon there was a small garden full of vegetables and flowers for Sita, and the three of them started to enjoy their simple life.

One day, soon after they had settled in, the sister of the terrible king of demons, Ravan, was strolling through the forest when she saw their cottage in a clearing by the river. Saroopanakha was a demoness and she had the power to change herself into any form she chose. She now transformed herself into a dazzling beauty, for otherwise anyone might have fainted at the sight of her real appearance.

Rama heard the sound of tinkling anklets and, looking up, saw in front of him this unbelievably lovely-looking woman. As soon as Saroopanakha met his gaze, she fell hopelessly in love with the handsome Rama; and, as her nature was completely crude and charmless, she boldly told him of her feelings.

'I want to marry you,' she said in dulcet tones; 'and because I am the sister of the great Ravan, I have all kinds of magical powers. I can give you anything you want. Come, let us rule the world together, you and I,' she simpered.

Rama thanked her politely and explained that he was already married to the most beautiful of all women, Sita.

'Oh, what does that matter?' Saroopanakha replied airily. 'You can leave her and come with me instead. What, is that her, gathering firewood under the trees? What a puny little thing!'

When she had been pestering Rama for quite a while, and he saw that his lack of interest was having no effect on her, he said jokingly: 'I really am married, but my handsome younger brother, Lakshman, might be interested in you. Why don't you ask him?'

Lakshman, of course, also rebuffed Saroopanakha's offers, after which she lost all patience. She made a rush at Sita to attack her with her long fingernails, and at that very instant she was changed back into her original, hideous form. Wild-haired, red-eyed, fanged and taloned, she was a revolting sight. Her hot, poisonous breath fouled the clean air and Sita screamed with terror. Lakshman ran to her defence. With two blows of his sword he sliced off Saroopanakha's ears, and with another he sliced off her nose. Humiliated and howling in anguish, Saroopanakha fled from Panchavati, shrieking that she would be back to take revenge.

Screaming and crying, Saroopanakha ran to her brother, Khara, who was a younger brother of Ravan. Khara had a stronghold in the Dandak forest and, after the defeat of Mareech and Subahu, had become the principal trouble-maker in that region. He called fourteen of his best soldiers and told them to get rid of Rama and Lakshman once and for all and to bring back Sita as a prisoner. But even fourteen cunning demons didn't stand a chance against Rama and Lakshman and their divine weapons.

In the end Khara had to send his entire army to fight the two brothers, but every single demon in his army was killed by the princes. Now Khara himself came to face Rama and Lakshman. He hurled his magic mace at them, but a deadly stream of arrows from the brothers' bows shattered it into tiny pieces. Snarling with fury, Khara next uprooted a tree and flung it at them. It splintered into matchsticks under their arrows. Rama was a fair fighter, but now he saw it was time to finish off his opponent, and a perfectly aimed arrow soon put an end to Khara.

Only one of his demons had survived the massacre, and he fled in panic to Lanka. Taking his sorry tale to the great Ravan, the demon begged him to come and do something about King Dasharath's two warrior sons. 'Rama is a real threat to our race. Besides killing

Khara, he has disfigured your sister, Saroopanakha. And all she did was fall in love with him.'

Saroopanakha, who had also come with her complaint, hissed, 'I hate that puny little Sita-wife of his.' She turned to her brother. 'Sita is just to your taste. A nice little morsel she'd make for me, but you would enjoy her company in your palace. She is rather lovely.' Saroopanakha had touched Ravan's weak spot, because he loved to collect wives. 'I think,' his witch-like sister went on, 'that you should kidnap her. She would easily be the most beautiful woman in your collection.'

Ravan thought long and hard: he was quite determined to get his revenge. At last, having planned a devilish scheme in his mind, he called for his flying chariot, which was called Pushpakvimaan, and went to pay a visit to Mareech. Some years before, Rama's discus had dumped Mareech in the ocean. Since then the demon had changed his ways and was now living a quiet life, trying to repent of his sins. As he sat under a forest tree, praying, he felt a huge shadow come between him and the sun. He opened his eyes and there, in front of him, was his old master, Ravan.

8 The Golden Deer

Ravan curtly told Mareech to get up as he had a job for him. 'I am going to finish off the Ikshvaku dynasty, and I need your help,' he said.

Mareech, who had first-hand knowledge of Rama and Lakshman's strength, was understandably alarmed. 'You cannot defeat them in battle,' he told Ravan.

'Who said anything about battle?' Ravan leered horribly. 'I'm going to carry away their prize jewel, Sita, for my own. Rama will be so upset that he won't be able to fight any more. That's when I'll finish him off; and his brother,' Ravan added, as an afterthought. 'You,' he pointed to the frightened Mareech, 'are going to disguise yourself as a golden deer. The prettiest deer that was ever seen.' He rubbed his twenty hands together. 'Your hoofs will glitter with blood-rubies and your hide will brindle with emeralds and diamonds. As you leap, tiny rainbows will spark from your tail.' He chuckled wickedly. 'No woman will be able to resist you – and no man either. You have to attract Sita's attention and draw Rama and Lakshman away from the cottage. I will do the rest.' His laughter was so sinister that the nearby trees let go their leaves with fear.

Mareech had no choice: either he disobeyed Ravan and died at his hands, or he obeyed him and would be killed by Rama and Lakshman. Without a great deal of enthusiasm he changed himself into a golden deer with a jewelled pattern in its hide. He paraded himself before Ravan and, after he had been approved of, he bounded away with a flying leap deep into the forest.

That morning Sita was gathering herbs and flowers in a glade near the cottage. Suddenly, from out of the corner of her eye, she glimpsed a swift flash of gold. She straightened up and saw the most delicate little golden deer nibbling the grass, a few feet away from her. It caught her glance with innocent, wide, brown eyes and skipped a little further away. Its movements illuminated the forest with flashes of molten sunshine. Tiny rainbows played around its tail and the most wonderfully coloured jewels threw lozenges of light in its wake.

'Rama, Lakshman! Come quick! Look, it must be a gift from the gods! Quick, do catch it before it disappears.' Lakshman dropped his bow, which he had been polishing, and Rama laid down his garden hoe. They saw the dazzling creature bounding from one glade to another, looking at them almost challengingly every now and then.

'Oh Rama, I must have it – do get it for me!' cried Sita.

'No, Rama,' Lakshman warned. 'Don't, it could be a demon in disguise.'

But Sita wanted the deer so badly that Rama couldn't resist trying to please her; she had never asked for anything for herself and had put up with so many hardships during the exile. He wanted to give her a present, so he fetched his bow and a quiverful of arrows.

'Stay here and look after Sita,' he told his brother. 'Don't leave her for a minute.' The deer shot another glance that seemed to dare him to follow it, then sprang further into the forest with Rama in full chase.

It led him a merry dance, skipping behind trees, jumping over streams and dodging around the under-growth. When it had lured Rama miles away from the cottage, it climbed up a bank and presented itself as a sitting target. Rama took aim and easily brought down the creature. At once it let out a terrible cry which echoed all through the forest: 'Oh, Sita, oh, Lakshman!' Having completed his master's instructions, the deer (who was really Mareech) died.

When he heard the human-sounding voice, Rama knew he had been tricked and he hit the palm of his hand against his forehead in frustration. 'I hope Lakshman stays with Sita and doesn't come looking for me,' he thought. 'The cry sounded just like my voice.'

Meanwhile Sita and Lakshman had heard the call for help, just as they were meant to. 'It's Rama! He's in trouble! Go immediately and find him,' cried Sita.

Lakshman was uneasy. 'I was told to stay by your side, and that is what I'm going to do,' he said firmly.

'Will you let your brother die? Have you no sense of duty? What if he is injured and bleeding to death? Go immediately, please, and bring my Rama back to me so I can take care of his wounds,' Sita pleaded with tears in her eyes so that Lakshman could not refuse.

He agreed to go, but before going he warned Sita not to move outside the cottage garden. With the tip of his bow he drew a ring round the cottage in the dust. 'Stay inside this,' he yelled, sprinting in the direction of the cry.

Sita felt guilty and uneasy and she wished she

hadn't made Rama chase after the deer. Lakshman knew that Rama had been tricked and he was torn between rescuing Rama and guarding Sita.

Rama was now certain that a plan was unfolding to harm all three of them, especially Sita. He sped back home to try and avert the disaster.

A hushed silence now descended into the clearing, as though all the forest creatures were holding their breath. The woodpecker stopped his tapping, squirrels scampered to safety and bees burrowed into the mouths of flowers. Even the wind dropped, so as to warn Sita of danger. But her mind was too full of Rama and, when a stranger suddenly appeared in front of the cottage, she was caught off guard.

It was an old man, dressed in the simple ochre-coloured clothes of a hermit. With his long beard, topknot, begging bowl and staff he looked harmless enough.

Sita's kindly instincts made her ask if he would like something to eat and drink. The old man thanked her and said he would wait outside. Sita quickly heated the food which she had prepared earlier that morning. When she took out the saucepan and a jar of water, the old hermit held out his bowl. It was just out of her reach, so she asked him to come forward. She had remembered what Lakshman had told her, that she must not move outside the magic circle. With a sad smile the hermit said, 'Are you afraid of an old man like me? You should respect my age and serve me properly. Come a little closer.'

Sita felt she could trust the elderly man, so she moved forward a little to fill his bowl, when he suddenly gripped her wrist like an iron manacle. Horrified, she exclaimed, 'What are you doing?'

'Taking you with me to Lanka, where you will be my queen!' he exulted. Ravan's hermit disguise fell away to reveal the ten-headed, twenty-armed king of demons. His dark skin shone like polished bronze, his red eyes glittered in triumph as he picked up his prize in one of his many arms and carried her to his waiting chariot. All the blood seemed to leave her body as Sita screamed and shouted for help, but there was no one to hear her.

9 The Abduction

Rama and Lakshman were still far away, and Sita's sobs and cries could not reach them. But someone did hear her, and that was Jatayu. The ancient bird was dozing on the branch of a mango tree when the noise of Sita's cries startled him awake. He looked down from his perch and saw Ravan come crashing through the undergrowth, with his victim struggling to free herself from his many arms, intending to carry her to his flying chariot, which was waiting for him.

'Stop! How dare you!' the old bird called from his treetop. 'Leave her at once. That is the Princess Sita, daughter of King Janak, daughter-in-law of my old friend King Dasharath and the wife of Prince Rama of Ayodhya.'

Ravan paid no attention as he quickly bundled his victim into the chariot, which was driven by gargoyle-faced donkeys and a hideously ugly demon charioteer. The magically powered vehicle rose into the air.

'Help me, help me!' cried Sita. 'Tell Rama that Ravan, the king of Lanka, has kidnapped me!' With a powerful push upwards, Jatayu spread his enormous wings and took flight. There was a resounding crash as he met the chariot in mid-air. Like a hurricane colliding with a storm cloud, the king of the eagles and the king of demons clashed, hundreds of feet above the ground. Jatayu attacked Ravan with his talons, tearing out chunks of flesh with his beak, but Ravan aimed a quiverful of poisonous serpents at the brave bird. Before the venom had a chance to circulate through his bloodstream, Jatayu swiped with his great wings at Ravan's charioteer. The demon lost his balance and was pulled down by gravity, to be smashed to pieces down below. With a roar, Ravan then slashed at Jatayu's wings with his sword and severed them from his torso. Jatayu's blood showered the air as his magnificent wings fell to the ground, and the mighty bird hurtled down after them, mortally wounded.

Sita's voice grew fainter and fainter as the chariot sped away, 'Tell Rama, tell Rama!' The cry echoed in the bird's ears and a drift of flower petals floated gently down and settled on his old head. Sita was scattering the flowers from her garland as she was transported further and further away from the Dandak forest.

By the time Rama and Lakshman finally caught up with each other, Sita had been whisked away to far-off Lanka and they had no idea what had happened to her. Abandoning the cottage, the brothers set off to search for any clue that might lead them to her. Sita's companions, the forest creatures, came out of their hiding-places, running here and there, chattering and chirruping. They hopped up and down and ran in circles round Rama, trying to tell him what they had seen, but they could not speak a human language and they looked on in frustration as Rama and Lakshman tried to decide which direction to take.

Noticing a freshly broken branch here and a foot-print over there, the brothers managed to follow a trail in the right direction. At last, panting and panic-stricken, they arrived at the scene of the battle between Jatayu and Ravan. Jatayu was lying in a pool of blood, soft heaps of his own feathers blowing all around his last resting place.

Feebly he raised his head when he heard Rama's voice, and told him to head south. 'I did all I could, but I am so old, so useless. I promised I would guard her but, when the time came, I let you down. Please forgive me,' he said, collapsing again with the effort of trying to talk. 'Ravan has carried away your Sita. These are dark times, but you will find her again one day and all will be well.'

Rama cradled Jatayu's wounded head in his arms and stroked the crippled body until the bird gave up his life. Then Rama and Lakshman said funeral prayers for Jatayu and cremated him. Rama had not been able to say the prayers for his own father's funeral, but he so admired Jatayu that he poured all his respect into the ceremony for the regal bird as he put his soul into the care of the gods.

Hindus venerate Jatayu for his defence of Sita. His heroism in the unequal battle with Ravan is seen as an example of how one should defend what is right, whatever the obstacles.

10 Sita's Imprisonment

After they had said goodbye to Jatayu, the princes were given some help along the way, but it came in a most unexpected form. As they headed in a southerly direction, they were suddenly pounced upon by a ferocious-looking monster with a single eye in the middle of his barrel-shaped chest. On either side of his torso hung a massive arm, each one the thickness of a log. He advanced towards them in a threatening manner which signalled trouble.

'You deal with one of his arms and I'll cut off the other,' Rama directed Lakshman. With one blow from Rama to the left and one blow by Lakshman to the right, both the monster's arms dropped off like tree branches felled by a woodcutter. To the brothers' great astonishment, the armless creature reacted to his disfigurement by bowing low and informing them that because of his sinful deeds he had been placed under a curse by the gods. He had been told that the curse would be broken only when Rama and Lakshman came and cut off his arms. 'I am still not quite free. Now you have to set fire to me,' he said, kneeling before them in submission.

Rama looked at Lakshman, wondering what would happen next, but he picked up some dry brushwood and arranged it into a pile. Lakshman gathered a few dead branches and set the bonfire alight. The flames licked round the armless monster and soon burnt him to cinders. Then, as soon as the fire began to subside, from the smoking embers emerged another and very different, ethereal being. This creature was of a different order from the one before – graceful and beauteous to look at.

'Thank you for freeing me,' he cried. 'Now I am myself once more! Prince Rama, you will find your Sita again, but you must do it with the help of Sugriv, who lives across the River Pampa in Rishyamukh hill. He is a prince of the monkey kingdom and has been exiled by his brother, Bali. Make friends with him, and he will help you.' Then, with a wave of his hand, he disappeared into the sky.

Now that Rama and Lakshman had a firm idea as

to where to begin their search, their steps took a lighter tread. The walk through the Pampa valley to Rishyamukh led them through a beautiful valley covered in flowering shrubs and creepers. Rama plucked a deep pink hibiscus flower and held it to the light. Its rich colour and transparent petals glowed like the bloom on Sita's cheeks. He became silent and moody as he thought of his beloved wife. His straight shoulders sagged and he began to drag his feet as he walked. Every few minutes he would stop, stare at the ground and sigh heavily. Lakshman had not seen him so dejected before. He put his arm round Rama to remind him that he was not alone. When that didn't work, he made Rama sit down in the shade of a tree and told him that difficulties and hardship should not make him give up hope. 'Action, brother, action is what we need. Come, walk faster, because that will bring us closer to Sugriv, who is going to help us to find Sita.'

Meanwhile, Ravan's chariot had landed in his palace gardens, and all his servants ran to take their orders from him. He was gentle with Sita at first because he wanted to make a good impression. 'All my servants will do anything you want. Come and look at my palace, my jewels and my treasures – they are yours if you marry me and leave your disinherited prince. He

cannot give you anything except a miserable life —
and, of course, he is never going to find you.'

'I will have nothing to do with you, Ravan,' Sita
answered. 'Do you think you can compare yourself to
my dear Rama? It's like a crow thinking he looks like
a swan!' She picked a blade of grass and laid it on the
ground. 'Even that little piece of grass divides us. We
come from different worlds and your demon nature
and my human nature have nothing in common.'

Ravan bristled with anger and hurt pride, because
he had fallen in love with Sita. He had never come
across such a combination of beauty and goodness
before. 'If you will not have me now, then I give you
twelve months to consider my offer. If you do not
marry me by then, I'm afraid I'll have to kill you and
give you to my demons for breakfast.'

By now Sita was exhausted, and she could not help
tears welling up and splashing down her face. But she
was the daughter of a warrior king and the wife of a
warrior prince, and she did not want her enemy
enjoying the sight of her weakness. She covered her
head with the end of her garment so that Ravan
would not see her crying.

'Take her to the Ashok Garden,' bellowed her
kidnapper, 'and keep a close watch on her. Do not be
too cruel, but do not be kind either. She is a prisoner
until she comes to her senses and decides to marry

72

me.' Ravan handed her over to his ogresses, who pushed, pinched and shoved her all the way to her new home in the ashok grove.

11 Sugriv, Bali and Hanuman

The king of the monkey kingdom, Sugriv, was living in the forests below the hill of Rishya-mukh. With him were his loyal followers, including a monkey whose father had been the god of the wind. The name of this extraordinary monkey was Hanuman, and he was famous for his incredible strength and his ability to change his shape and size whenever he wished. Hanuman spotted Rama and Lakshman as they entered the forest looking for Sugriv, and he approached them disguised as a holy man. He greeted them politely and, because he was friendly and well-spoken, Rama warmed to him. As soon as they had found out about one another and had decided that they could trust each other, Hanuman told them who

74

he really was. He assumed his monkey body, covered with golden brown fur. He had a long, graceful tail which curled in a crook and his wise, amber-coloured eyes were set in a kind, intelligent face. Leading the way through the forest, he clambered up the hill and conducted them to his king. Sugriv also immediately took to Rama and Lakshman and agreed to help them find Sita.

'But I need to tell you a little of my sad story,' Sugriv explained. 'My older brother, whom I loved dearly, has exiled me from my home and is now married to my wife, the queen of the monkeys. It is all due to a tragic misunderstanding. Many years ago, a demon entered our palace in Kishkindha, the capital, and challenged my brother, King Bali, to a duel. As the duel became more and more fierce, the demon ran away and hid in a hillside cave. Bali chased him, after telling me to wait by the entrance to the cave. I stood guard for a long, long time and then, to my despair, I heard groans coming from inside which sounded as though Bali had been fatally injured. I wanted to stop the demon from getting out and returning to destroy Kishkindha, so I quickly rolled a huge rock against the mouth of the cave. I thought Bali had died fighting, and I allowed the councillors to crown me king of the monkeys. But Bali had not died. He came out of the cave, after killing the demon, and accused me of imprisoning him inside it in order to take over the throne.

'I had not acted from bad motives, but he was so angry with me that he did not listen and drove me out of Kishkindha. If I help you to find Sita, will you in return help me to go back to my kingdom? Will you help me to overcome Bali?'

Rama gave him his promise, since he felt that Sugriv had been treated unfairly. Rama, too, had been exiled, from Ayodhya, but he had left for quite a different reason: in order not to dishonour his father's promise. Everyone had begged him not to go because they knew how Kaikeyi had trapped Dasharath into promising her a favour; a favour which was completely unjust. Only Rama had chosen to make the sacrifice that would keep his father's name intact. He had not actually been forced to leave. His brother, Bharat, was only a reluctant caretaker until Rama came back to rule over Koshal. Rama thought of the deep love and trust between himself and Bharat and felt very sorry for Sugriv, whose brother had not given him the benefit of the doubt.

To seal their agreement, Rama, Lakshman, Sugriv and Hanuman decided to make a pact of friendship. Then Sugriv showed Rama a pair of anklets which had fallen from the sky not long before their arrival.

'I saw a chariot in the sky. It swept by like a fiery-tailed comet, but in its wake came the sound of a lady weeping. She must have thrown down this jewellery, hoping that a friend would pick it up and realize she had passed this way.'

It was a moment of happy optimism for Rama. He held the anklets in his hand and prayed for his wife's safety.

At that very moment, in far-off Lanka, Sita's left eyelid throbbed. A breath of hope came to her like a soft breeze from the trees in Ravan's garden, for the throbbing of the left eyelid is a good omen.

Sugriv could not be of much help to Rama without the resources of the monkey army, and that was possible only if he could become the commander-in-chief once again. As his brother had refused to have any more to do with him, Sugriv had no alternative but to get his brother out of the way so that he could return home and control the army. Reluctantly he challenged Bali to a combat.

Bali was completely incensed by his brother's nerve. He rushed out of his palace and started wrestling with Sugriv. The monkey brothers rolled around in the mud, getting more and more angry and worked up. Their eyes flashed, their fur flew, their tails sparked with electric tension and their snarls sent shivers of fear into the bystanders. Rama was waiting on one side with his magic bow and arrows. He had promised to defend Sugriv, but in the confusion of the wrestling match it was difficult to make out which was Bali and which was Sugriv. Rama aimed this way and that but couldn't tell at whom to fire the shot. Bali lassoed his tail round Sugriv, picked him up and threw him to the ground. Sugriv aimed a kick at Bali and jumped on him, trying to pin his arms round his back. But Bali shook him off easily, lifted him up, spun him around and dropped him heavily. Sugriv was completely winded and lost the first round of the fight. When he limped away, Lakshman wound a wreath made of green creepers round his neck to help Rama distinguish between the two monkey brothers. This time Rama's arrow found its mark and Bali fell back, mortally wounded.

He knew he was dying and with every weakening breath his anger against his brother evaporated. 'We could have been friends,' he lamented. 'We could have shared the throne between us.'

Sugriv's anger also disappeared, and he wept, because he loved Bali. He blamed himself for having been too hasty in taking over as king after Bali had failed to re-emerge from the cave. 'Your anger and my impatience have led to this tragic end,' he repented. 'Forgive me, my brother!'

'I forgive you. Look after my family and be especially kind to my son, Angad,' Bali whispered as his eyes closed in the sleep from which he would never waken.

Once Sugriv had been crowned king again, he began to live a riotous life. Every night he celebrated his return home with a party; serious matters could wait for a while. He seemed to have forgotten his promise to Rama and Lakshman. By then the rainy season had begun and any kind of military action would be out of the question for several months. Rain flooded the valley and brought avalanches of mud and rocks down the hillsides. All day and all night the trees dripped like waterfalls. Sugriv stayed inside the palace in Kishkindha, and Rama and Lakshman camped in a dry cave near by. The dismal weather resulted in too much time to think and miss the presence of Sita, and Rama started to become very sad and depressed.

Lakshman did his best to try and cheer him up, but at last he decided that Sugriv needed to be taught a lesson. The rains had at last ended, there was no excuse now for inaction. Lakshman was tired of waiting. Seething with impatience and annoyance, he made his way to the palace to give Sugriv a piece of his mind.

He waited by the palace gates and fingered his

bowstring. Hearing the warning, Hanuman, who was very embarrassed by Sugriv's behaviour, hurried to try and rouse him from his drunken stupor. 'You swore eternal friendship to Rama and Lakshman, and now you are running away from your duty!'

Sugriv, who had not meant any offence, managed to collect his wits and sent his courtiers to escort Lakshman inside. He told him he was very sorry, but he hadn't realized the passage of time. He was going to make amends at once by summoning the entire army as the first step towards organizing his monkeys in the promised search for Sita.

The monkeys came from all four corners of the earth: from the swamps of the eastern regions, from the small, jewel-like islands of Java and Sumatra, from the great snowy mountains in the north, the parched deserts of the east and west, and from the southern jungles. Sugriv sent eight battalions out to look for Sita. They were told to cover the four corners of the earth and were given a month to report back.

Hanuman was singled out for special orders by Sugriv. 'Do not spare yourself. Use every charm, every power, to discover her whereabouts. If anyone in the whole world is able to find her, you are.'

Rama gave Hanuman his gold signet ring to show to Sita. 'She will know you are my messenger. Go swiftly, son of the wind, and bring her back to me.'

They waved farewell as Hanuman and Angad, together with some trusted monkey soldiers, marched away with their heads held high and their tails proudly aloft. Jambuvan, a bear of great wisdom, accompanied them, plodding along behind the monkey procession.

12 Hanuman's Adventures

Travelling southwards proved to be full of dangers and deadly obstacles for Hanuman and his friends. Demons and ogres leapt into their path and threatened to swallow them alive; food was not always at hand, and sometimes fresh water seemed to be scarcer than the nectar of the gods. At the end of one very difficult stretch, which had led them through a burning hot desert, they saw a cool green cave, with delicious, life-giving water trickling from the walls. With whoops of joy they scampered inside and were met by musky, perfume-laden breezes blowing from far within.

Linking hands, they moved deeper into the mysterious darkness. There was nothing to guide them except their animal vision. They brushed past feathery ferns and splashed through rock pools until, at last, the blackness started to melt into light and they emerged from the cave to find themselves in a grove of mango trees. Scarlet parrots flitted about, pecking at ripe fruit, while butterflies settled on scented flowers. In the distance they could see a city glittering in the sunshine with silver and precious stones, and outside its walls an old woman sat, praying, on a deerskin mat.

Hanuman greeted her with his usual great politeness, whereupon she invited them to eat and drink their fill. The monkeys were famished, so they crammed as many golden-fleshed mangoes into their mouths as their stomachs would hold. When they were full, the old woman told them that they would never be able to leave that country because they would never find the cave again.

However, once she had heard the sad story of Rama, Sita and Lakshman, she understood the nature of their special mission and gave them permission to go their way. She closed her eyes, concentrated hard and, by strength of a special prayer, was able to propel them into their own world through the magic cave.

Flying through time and space, the friends landed

very far away on a distant seashore, with the incoming tide curling round their feet. The great open sky yawned above them and the horizon stretched to infinity in the distance. Hanuman looked shorewards and saw that the trees and bushes in the hinterland had come into fresh new leaf. It was spring and they had already been away from Kishkindha for many months. He covered his eyes in shame and said to Angad, 'I have already failed the test. We were given a month for our search, but we must have spent many weeks in the country of the cave, because spring is already here.'

The other monkeys and Jambuvan also felt they had let down King Sugriv and Rama. Angad was sure that Sugriv would punish them with death. 'There is no point in going back home,' he concluded sadly. 'Either we go back to the cave into the magic country, or we fast to death.'

The monkeys huddled together, arguing and chattering about their next step; they created such a disturbance that they attracted the attention of a very large bird who was thinking about his next meal. The bird's name was Sampati and he was the brother of the heroic Jatayu who had valiantly tried to defend Sita. When he had been young and energetic, he and Jatayu had held a competition to see who could fly up highest in the sky. Higher and higher they flew, until

Jatayu came so close to the sun that he would surely have been scorched to a cinder. With a huge effort, Sampati flew above him and shielded him from the fierce heat. Jatayu was saved, but Sampati's wings were burnt off. Poor Sampati fell like a lead weight down on to a small hill near the seashore and was never able to move very far again. It was difficult for him to hunt for food and he was always hungry.

Now, when he saw the monkeys, he also saw his next meal. As he poised himself to attack, he heard them telling the whole story of Rama and Sita. Suddenly he heard the name of his own brother, Jatayu. The monkeys had come to the part of the story where Sampati's brother had tried to save Princess Sita. 'What's that, what's that I hear? Tell me about Jatayu. Where is he and how can I find him?' he cried, hobbling over to the monkey band. When the monkeys saw the sad old eagle, they went to him, led him down the hill and gently broke the news of Jatayu's end. Sampati mourned for a long time, but when his eyes were dry again he looked at them directly. 'I may be old and infirm, but my eyes are still young and I am able to see for miles and miles. I will try to help you by looking to see what I can find.' He gazed with his eagle eyes for a long time across the ocean. At last he spoke. 'I see the Princess Sita. She is sorrowing, but she is safe. Ravan has imprisoned her in the Ashok Garden near his palace.' As he was speaking, the most amazing thing began to happen: Sampati's wings started to grow again! Soft, downy feathers appeared on his stumps and grew into plumes, bigger and bigger, until his wings were back to their normal size. Then Sampati remembered a prophecy he had been told many years before: that when he helped Rama, he would get back his wings.

'To Lanka! To Lanka!' the monkeys shouted, thrilled that they had at last located Sita. But how were they going to get there?

Hanuman withdrew from the noisy band and climbed up the hill to meditate and think about their next move. He was sitting, lost in thought, when Jambuvan lumbered up behind him 'Do not think too long, Hanuman. Have you forgotten that you are the son of the wind god? You have been given all kinds of gifts, and your strength is beyond imagining. Perhaps, because you are so modest, you sometimes forget the things you are able to do. I remember when you were young you reached out for the sun because you thought it was an orange! You made a leap for it, as though it was a fruit growing on a tree. You are the only one amongst us who can leap as far as Lanka. Pray for power, pray for strength,' the wise old bear advised.

So Hanuman prayed with great concentration and

his body began to expand and grow, becoming filled with strength and buoyancy. He rested one foot on the hill and it created an earthquake. Landslides crashed down the sides, huge rocks went tumbling into the sea and all the nesting birds flew out of their trees, screeching with fear. Deer, squirrels, lions and panthers ran outside their lairs in alarm, and snakes and serpents swarmed out of their holes in panic.

Then, with one mighty spring, Hanuman jumped into the air and went roaring like a tornado in the direction of Lanka. As he sped onwards, high in the sky, his shadow coursed behind him on the surface of the water like a swift, dark ship. His friends watched as he grew smaller and smaller and finally disappeared over the endless horizon.

13 More Adventures

*O*ver the blue ocean he flew, marvelling at the white sea-horses, the patches of indigo where the water was deeper, the flying fish, dolphins and whales, and the turquoise and green coloured shallows. When he almost ran into a flock of seagulls he knew that Lanka was near. Soon land appeared, covered in coconut groves and banana plantations. Further inland Hanuman saw the rooftops and turrets of Ravan's city. It was elegantly laid out, with wide streets and spacious parks. From his bird's-eye view Hanuman saw the demon inhabitants going about their work and play like a colony of ants.

It would have been impossible to locate Sita from this height, so he decided to land on a nearby mountain and shrank himself down from a giant size to a small monkey no bigger than a cat. In his much-reduced form he was swinging nimbly from tree to tree on his way to the city gates when he heard the sound of heavy breathing, as though a wild boar was tracking him. He paused for a moment to listen when, to his dismay, a terrifying ghostly figure confronted him.

'No one gets by me,' it said in a rasping voice. 'How dare you try and sneak past the Guardian Spirit of Lanka? Who are you and what is your business?' The presence towered in front of the little monkey, but Hanuman simply pushed it aside with his left hand. Even though he was in a small-monkey form, his incredible strength knocked his opponent to the ground. To his surprise, when the spirit got up, it offered him no resistance. Instead it bowed and said, 'I was told that when a monkey threw me down it would be the beginning of the end for Ravan's kingdom. He is not my master and I am glad to know that his evil days are coming to an end. Go in peace and may you have success.'

The moon was up, and its silvery light made the landscape clearly visible. Keeping to the shadows, Hanuman entered the city, which was humming with activity. The inhabitants were all followers of Ravan. Some were tall and handsome, others were short and ugly. They had various kinds of features and skin colour and had been attracted to Lanka from all parts of the world. Warriors strode along dressed in full armour, while other people knelt in front of wayside shrines, worshipping their gods. Through the open windows of beautiful houses came the sounds of jingling anklets and music, song and revelry. Thoroughbred horses ridden by liveried servants highstepped past and ornately decorated elephants plodded through the streets.

Hanuman crept into houses to see how the people lived. There was a lot of merrymaking going on, with parties and concerts, eating and drinking, all in the most luxurious surroundings, full of extravagant comfort. He finally came to Ravan's palace, which was the most splendid of all, decorated with precious stones like cat's-eyes, topaz, lapis lazuli, turquoise and carnelian, and with silver and gold. He tiptoed through one courtyard after another overhung with trellised balconies and smothered in flowering creepers. In each of the rooms a beautiful woman lay sleeping, all of them the wives of Ravan, and none of them Sita. Ravan himself lay stretched out on an enormous golden bed like a colossal giant, and his snores shook the entire building.

Hanuman started to feel a little worried. If Sita was nowhere in the palace, where could she be? Was it possible that she had died of grief and longing? But surely he would have known instinctively if that had happened. A prickle of anxiety ran through his normally fearless being. He collected himself, concentrated hard and allowed his sixth sense to guide him outside the sleeping palace into the moonlit garden.

Dodging from shadow to shadow, he found himself in a part of the garden which was completely hidden by a copse of ashok trees. Through the rustle of leaves in the night breeze his ears caught the sound of someone weeping softly. Hanuman clambered on to a branch and from there he got his first glimpse of Sita. She was even more beautiful than Rama's description, although she was carelessly dressed, with her long hair twisted into a single plait which dangled below her waist. She had grown very thin, and even in the moonlight he could see she looked pale and wan. Her tears flowed copiously and he heard her soft voice lamenting, 'Rama, where are you? Have you forgotten your Sita?'

As he watched her, Hanuman wondered how he should make himself known to her. A sudden intrusion into her thoughts might frighten her. Besides, all round her lay the sleeping forms of demonesses who had been placed there by Ravan to guard her. As he was planning a strategy, the night started to melt into dawn and with it Hanuman heard the earth shake under the heavy footsteps of her captor advancing through the garden. Ravan was coming to gloat over his prisoner.

Ravan arrived in the ashok grove, refreshed after his night's sleep, and stood over Sita with his great arms akimbo. His ten heads and twenty eyes surveyed the scene in order to satisfy himself that she was being closely guarded. He was irritated to find her still in tears.

'Come, come,' he said cajolingly. 'What is there to cry about? You may have lost that no-good hermit husband of yours – after all, it is ten months now and he hasn't shown up – but you have me, don't you?' He preened his ten moustaches, some of them with his right hands and some with his left, so that his arms got jumbled up into an awkward tangle. 'Have you decided to stop this silly tragedy scene? I want to make you my chief wife and take you all over the world in my flying chariot. We will have a wonderful time and you will be queen of all my lands. Anything you could possibly want shall be yours. But you really must stop this nonsense and agree to marry me.'

Sita faced him and spoke with feeling. 'Why do you want what does not belong to you? Why do you insist on doing something which is evil in everyone's sight? You will never escape from Rama's anger. Listen! I can even now hear the twang of his bowstring as a warning to you! I will never marry you, but you still have time to escape the results of your wrong-doing. Let me go back to my husband and I am sure he will forgive you even now.'

Ravan's face turned dark red with rage. 'I gave you twelve months to decide, and only two are left. I warn you that, if you continue with your stubborn-ness, I shall have no choice but to give you over to the ogresses. The only use they have for you will be to serve you up for breakfast. They love human flesh and are waiting for me to deliver you to them. Remember, you have just sixty days to agree to my proposal.' He wagged ten right index fingers in warn-ing so that even the air whistled with fright. Then he turned around and walked away, back to his palace.

Sita fell into a fresh fit of despair as her wardresses danced round her in a grotesque display of triumph. 'We won't have to wait much longer to enjoy your flesh,' they screamed. Sita hid her face until they left her alone. It was at this point that Hanuman made his presence known to her.

From his perch in the ashok branch he began, very softly and gently, to chant the name of Rama. 'Rama . . . Rama . . . Rama . . .' Sita looked around, her face a mixture of astonishment and delight, and saw the little cat-sized monkey looking back at her with the kindest expression she had seen for a very long time.

14 Hanuman and Sita

At first Sita thought that Ravan had come in yet another disguise to torment her, so she covered her ears with her hands. But Hanuman kept speaking in a soothing voice from his branch and did not try to come any nearer. With his gift for poetic language he began to chant the story of Rama and Sita.

'King Dasharath of Ayodhya was a ruler
Known far and wide for his goodness, his power and
    majesty.
Commanding armies of soldiers who rode on elephants
    and horses,
Safeguarding his capital for his subjects,
Night and day they sang his praises.

Wealth and justice were their birthright and even greater
  joys lay ahead,
They looked forward to the future, when Prince Rama
  would be king
And continue his father's shining example.
But Rama, Sita and brother Lakshman were driven from
  the comfort of their home
To live in a forest full of dangers.
From place to place they wandered, doing good wherever
  they could,
And Rama and Lakshman destroyed the evil demons
That troubled the holy forest dwellers.
One unhappy day, the supremely evil Ravan
Sent a golden deer to lure Rama and Lakshman away
  from their cottage.
Poor Sita was left all alone.
Disguised as a holy man, Ravan carried her away
In his magic chariot to Lanka, where he bound her against
  her will.
Rama and Lakshman befriended Sugriv the monkey king
Exiled to the forest by his brother Bali.
Rama killed Bali and restored Sugriv to his throne.
In return Sugriv gathered a great army of monkeys,
Sending them to all four corners of the earth to find Sita,
But they returned empty-handed.
Then Hanuman flew over the vast ocean to Lanka
Where he has now found the Princess Sita
And wishes with all his heart to be of help to her.'

*

Sita clasped her hands with joy. 'If this is true,' she said, 'then my prayers have been answered. Come down from the tree and let me greet you properly.' Hanuman jumped down, folded his hands respectfully and told her he had come to rescue her.

'Ravan gave me twelve months to decide about my future as his wife. Only two are left, and when they are over I had made up my mind to kill myself. The gods have sent you just in time.'

'Dear Princess, your despair is now a thing of the past. Look, here is a ring which Rama sent for you. Do you recognize it?' He placed the signet ring on her open palm. 'Rama is waiting for you. Come, jump on my back and I will carry you to him over the ocean.'

Hanuman is the monkey with a valiant heart. Everyone in India loves him and prays to him for courage if they are faint-hearted. Because of him, even wild monkeys are treated with respect. Friendship and loyalty are two more qualities associated with him.

Sita thought for a while. 'No, my friend, that would not be right,' she said. 'The proper thing is for my husband Rama to come and take me away from here. He must act like the warrior he is and must get the credit for having rescued me. I know Rama, and I know he would want to punish Ravan for his sins. I think you should hurry back to him and tell him about the situation. Rama will march into Lanka at the head of the monkey army and he will completely destroy this arch-demon. But there is not much time left before I am fed to the demonesses, so please go, and don't delay a moment longer.'

However, Hanuman did not leave Lanka straight away. He felt it his duty to protect Sita from Ravan's attentions. He knew it was important to give her some courage and strength to keep hoping and not give up until Rama came to rescue her. Sitting very still, he cleared his mind of all thoughts and concentrated on a spell which once more made him into an enormous size, as tall as the trees in the Ashok Garden. Then, with calculated anger, he began to destroy the park which had been Sita's prison for ten months.

With a flick of his wrist he cracked the basins in which the fountains were playing. With a stamp of his foot he overturned the marble pavilions and summerhouses. He pulled up trees as if he were weeding a flowerbed and sent herds of deer scattering in all directions. The demonesses ran to the palace, screaming that a monster had devastated Ravan's favourite garden, but, since Sita was safe and well, he must be a friend of hers and therefore an enemy of his.

Ravan ground his teeth so that sparks shot out of

his mouth. He rolled his fearsome eyes and shouted for his soldiers to go and finish off the strange monkey who was as big as a tree. But within minutes Hanuman had made short work of them. He climbed on top of a building and gave a victory shout. 'Long live Rama! Long live Lakshman! They will be here soon to put an end to you all! Your days are numbered! We are going to raze your city to the ground!'

Ravan sent for his top general and commanded him to fight Hanuman. It did not take long for Hanuman to finish him off. Then two of Ravan's sons went into battle and showered a storm of arrows at Hanuman, but they only glanced off him harmlessly. Hanuman killed one of them, but he wanted to meet Ravan face to face and give him a last chance to release Sita, so, when the second son came out to face him, he pretended to be wounded by a feathered arrow and fell down with a dramatic crash. With loud whoops of triumph, the Lankans dragged him to Ravan and threw him down in front of their master.

15 Hanuman's Revenge and Return Home

As he lay sprawled at the feet of the demon king Hanuman examined the living colossus towering above him: the shining, dark skin, wrathful eyes, huge ears hung with golden hoops, and the gigantic chest bulging with muscle and sinew. Hanuman couldn't help being impressed by Ravan's physique.

He got to his feet and looked sternly at his enemy. 'My name is Hanuman, a subject of King Sugriv, friend and ally of Prince Rama of Ayodhya. You have stolen his wife, the Princess Sita, and are holding her prisoner in your palace gardens. I have come to Lanka to rescue the princess and I would like to take her back to her husband now. I am sure that Prince Rama will be fair and will not harm you if you release his wife. But I'm afraid that he will not spare you if you keep her here.'

But instead of listening to Hanuman's plea for good sense, Ravan's face took on a more thunderous aspect. In a voice rumbling with menace he roared, 'Kill him immediately!'

'Your Majesty, that isn't possible,' his chief minister pointed out. 'This fellow is the servant of a king — a mere messenger — and the rules of kingly behaviour say that people like him must not be put to death. After all, he is not to blame. He is only Rama's instrument, and your real enemy is Rama.'

Ravan looked scornfully at Sita's champion. 'If I had my way, I would have you tortured in my special torture-chamber until the last breath was squeezed from your hairy body. But I'm not going to let you get away without punishing you. You have caused a great deal of damage to my property and you have killed several valiant fighters, including my son.' He glared ferociously at Hanuman and chewed the ends of his many moustaches.

Then suddenly he let out a raucous laugh which set the chandeliers shivering and chiming with fear. Turning his huge bulk on its massive throne, he called a guard. 'Set fire to this intruder's tail,' he snapped viciously.

Ravan's servants wrapped the long golden tail with pieces of cloth, dipped it in melted butter and then set a match to it. Pushing Hanuman roughly in front of them, they paraded him through the streets. Everyone came running to look at the sight and started to make fun of the noble monkey.

In the Ashok Garden, Sita's demoness guardians cackled with glee. 'Your friend is on fire! Serve him right for daring to enter our land.' Hastily Sita made a small bonfire with dried leaves and twigs and prayed to the god of fire to protect Hanuman from burns.

Looking around at his blazing tail, Hanuman could not understand why he did not feel the effects of the fire, until he realized that the god of fire – who was a friend of his own father, the wind god – must have granted him special protection. He felt tremendously encouraged to have this reminder that the gods were on his side and he managed to break away from his guards. Running here and there, from building to building and house to house, blazing tail in hand, he torched whatever came his way. Soon the whole city was in flames and an outraged mob chased him while he raced nimbly to say goodbye to Sita.

'We will be back very soon, Rama and Lakshman, Sugriv and Angad, together with the entire monkey army and Jambuvan. Take heart, dear Princess, pray for us all and keep up your spirits!' Then, with a mighty spring, he rose into the air and was soon on his way back to his friends on the other side of the ocean.

This part of the Ramayana is recited as a sacred meditation whenever Hindus wish to pray for success in a difficult situation. The story of Hanuman's boldness in the face of danger is seen as an example of faith and determination against odds.

Across the water, on the opposite shore, Jambuvan the bear and the other monkeys had been camping on the beach, watching the sky and waiting anxiously for Hanuman's return. They saw him coming from a long way off, a tiny dot on the horizon which grew bigger and bigger until they could see Hanuman's golden limbs and his proud tail streaming behind him.

As soon as he had landed, they surrounded him, excitedly demanding to know his news and whether he had found Sita.

'Sita is found and for the time being she is safe; but only for the time being. As each hour ticks by, the danger to her person increases.' Then Hanuman sat down with his friends and told them the entire story of his adventures, beginning with his encounter with the Spirit of Lanka to the way he ran here and there setting fire to Ravan's capital. When he had finished, everyone cheered and clapped.

Hanuman held up a hand for silence. 'We must make a decision. We can go back to Lanka, all of us, and carry out the rescue. It would be possible for us to wipe out the entire demon race and bring Princess Sita back to Rama in Kishkindha. You, Angad, are a great warrior, so are you, Neel and you, Panas.' He named all the monkeys one by one. He then looked at Jambuvan. 'As for you, the demons will tremble when they see you.' He addressed the assembly once again: 'Come, what do you think we should do?'

Angad, stepson of Sugriv, jumped up, clenching a fist in the air. 'Let's go now!' he shouted. 'I can't wait to give Ravan the punishment he so richly deserves. I'm sure I can kill him all by myself!' The monkeys cheered even louder.

Jambuvan, the wise old bear, then got to his feet and said, 'I am sure we should go by Sita's wishes. I think we need to get back to Rama as quickly as possible and give him the news that she is alive. Surely Rama would like to fetch her from Lanka himself. He would want to vanquish Ravan with his own hands and show the world that evil can never win against good.'

Having heard the two arguments, everyone decided

that Jambuvan's was the better plan, and with Hanuman's help they rose up in the air and flew like a squadron of birds back to their own country.

They landed in Sugriv's private park near his palace. The instant they felt the familiar ground of home under their feet, relief and joy replaced their anxiety and fear. Their mission had been successful and not one body had been lost on the way. They knew that Rama and Lakshman's pleasure was going to be beyond description and that Ravan would soon be defeated. Letting out great whoops of happiness, they started dancing around, chasing each other through the trees, chattering and laughing. They picked the just-ripening mangoes and bananas and pelted each other with the fruit. So unruly was their behaviour that they uprooted flowers and bushes and tossed them around because they were unable to control their excitement.

Sugriv's head gardener went running to the throne room. 'Your majesty, a horde of monkeys, including your stepson, Angad, has ransacked your favourite garden. They are creating havoc out there. Order them to stop behaving in such a wild fashion!'

When Sugriv heard this, instead of becoming angry, a smile of delight spread across his face. He knew that

Hanuman had come back with good news from Lanka, and he sent for Rama and Lakshman so he could tell them the tidings they had been longing to hear.

16 Conferences of War

*L*ike a starving man who sees a table laden with delicious food and drink, feasting first with his eyes, then with his nose, and finally sitting down to fill his stomach, so Rama questioned Hanuman about Sita.

'Tell me how she looked. Was her face very sad when you spied her from your tree? And when she saw you, how did she appear then? Describe what happened after you told her who had sent you. Is she being treated with respect? Does she have clean clothes to wear, and has she grown pale and thin?'

Hanuman recounted his impressions to Rama, who persisted with more questions.

'Did the Princess Sita ask after me frequently? Did

she enquire after my brother, Lakshman, as well? She is full of courage, but surely she must be a little frightened by now. Tell me, Hanuman!'

Once his curiosity and longing to know every detail about his wife were exhausted, Rama sat down, weary with the knowledge of all her sufferings. Then he made Hanuman tell him the entire story from beginning to end. When he heard it through all over again, Rama asked him to repeat it so he could savour each word and phrase one more time.

Hanuman said, 'I have several messages for you. Princess Sita asked me to remind you of the time when a crow perched on her shoulder as she was sleeping in the forecourt of your cottage. She also remembered the occasion when you both went for a walk in the forest and the sweat on her forehead dissolved her red tilak mark; of how you crushed a rock to a fine red powder and made a fresh mark for her.' He was pleased to see Rama smile as he thought about those happy times they had had together.

Hanuman took a jewel from a small pouch round his neck and placed it in Rama's hand. 'She said her ornament would keep you company until you were together again.'

Rama gazed lovingly at the jewel which his wife had worn on her head and promised himself that it would not be long now before he would look on her dear face again. He embraced Hanuman warmly and thanked him from the bottom of his heart for his friendship and for everything he had done for Sita.

Meanwhile Sugriv had started drilling his monkey army, preparing it for the march to Lanka. The monkeys were in high spirits, having heard all about Hanuman's exploits from Angad and Jambuvan. They stepped out, right feet forward as this was considered to be lucky. Right left, right left, they marched to a victory song, leading the way southwards to the tip of the peninsula from where they would all cross over to the territory of the demon king.

All this while, Ravan had been making his own preparations. He first called a council of war to discuss what should be done in the aftermath of Hanuman's destruction of his capital. His throne room hummed and buzzed with rumours as his ministers whispered their fears and opinions to one another. It was an awe-inspiring sight, with the demon king seated in majesty on an agate throne and his advisers, dressed in their finery, gathered round him. Great mirrors made of highly polished silver reflected the yellow flames of the oil lamps and the rich red tapestries which covered the walls and floor. The air was heavy with anxiety. Ravan raised his hands for silence and spoke. 'Rama is now our sworn enemy. He will definitely try to cross the sea to get Sita back, and we must be able to defend our city. What are the weaknesses in our army? How can we be ready and alert for an attack?'

One after another, his generals stood up and promised him their support. All together they roared, 'We will make mincemeat of Rama and Lakshman and their silly monkey army!'

Only Vibhishan, Ravan's younger brother, stayed silent, thinking. He waited, chin in hand, until Ravan's council members had finished shouting their brave words. Then he stood up and addressed Ravan soberly. 'You are my brother and I am very fond of you,' he began, 'but I cannot flatter you like the others. I am sure you know in your heart that kidnapping Sita was very wrong. If you hated what Rama did to our sister, Saroopanakha, you should have challenged him directly to a fight, not gone behind his back and carried away his wife. No good can come of this deed. Ever since Sita arrived in Lanka, things have gone badly. There are bad omens everywhere: cows have stopped giving milk, our horses have fallen sick and crows perch on rooftops cawing all day long. Dogs roam the streets, licking the food left for our gods in shrines, and vultures are circling the sky from dawn to dusk. These are signs that always come before terrible things happen. Only you can change destiny by taking Sita back to Rama and putting aside your warlike intentions.'

Then Ravan's other brother, Kumbhkarna, stood up. He was a great sleepy fellow who preferred his bed to being active, but he was intensely loyal to Ravan. 'I agree with my younger brother that what you did was wrong.' He paused for a few seconds. 'But I have decided to support you through thick and thin, and I will fight every battle on your side and we will win!' He sat down again, worn out with the effort of saying a few sentences.

Now it was Indrajit's turn. Indrajit was Ravan's son, and he also defended his father against Vibhishan's wise advice. 'I think my uncle Vibhishan is a traitor! If he thinks Rama is so wonderful, why doesn't he go and join his side instead of sniping at my revered father?'

Vibhishan looked at the proud faces of his clansmen and saw that nothing would now change Ravan's mind. He no longer had any wish to be part of the demon way of life. He had seen the difference between right and wrong and was determined to follow his own conscience, so he left the council chamber without saying another word and went home. Before the day was out, he had given away his possessions and, using his magic powers, he propelled himself up into the sky and started to fly in the direction which would lead him to Rama and the monkey army.

Rama, Lakshman, Hanuman, Sugriv, Angad, Jambu-van and all the others had by now arrived at the seashore. The army had set up camp and the monkeys were scurrying around gathering firewood to cook the evening meal. All at once the setting sun beamed a slanting ray off the metal armour of Vibhishan as he hovered in the sky above them. It was a strange and dazzling sight as Ravan's brother remained suspended in the air, waiting to see whether it would be safe for him to land.

'I am Vibhishan,' he shouted, 'Ravan's brother. I have come to seek refuge with Rama. I have finished with my brother and I want to join your side.'

Some of Rama's friends urged him not to trust the demon king's brother, others wondered whether he was sincere. But Rama was a person who was always ready to forgive; he put down his bow and arrows and allowed the stranger to land on the ground. Finally it was Hanuman's advice that carried the day. 'I think we can read a person's intentions from his face. Vibhishan doesn't look as if he has anything to hide.'

Sugriv was less certain. 'But should we trust a man who betrays his own brother?' he asked.

'Not everyone is fortunate enough to have a

completely blameless and trustworthy brother like Bharat,' said Rama, looking at Lakshman with a smile. Both of them were thinking of the quarrel between Sugriv and Bali and how those two had become enemies. Rama spoke. 'Let Vibhishan come down and join our army. It is never too late for anyone to repent and turn to the right way.'

So Ravan's brother alighted on the ground in front of Rama, threw down his weapons and became an ally of his own brother's foes.

17 The War Against Ravan

*A*lthough Ravan had plenty of support from his other brother, Kumbhkarna, his sons and his generals, Vibhishan's desertion left him feeling a little uneasy. He paced around restlessly in his throne room, thinking with all his ten heads. One of the best ways to destroy an enemy force was to try and break it up. Ravan thought that if he could get Sugriv the money king on his side, then Rama and his friends would be much weaker.

He called one of his demons, Shuka, changed him into a parrot and sent him to Sugriv with a message. 'Tell Sugriv that I want him on my side. We are both kings and should help one another.'

But when Sugriv heard what the parrot had to say,

he threw back his head and laughed. He tapped Shuka's beak and said, 'Tell your king that I will never be a friend of his.'

The monkeys pulled Shuka's feathers and wanted to torture him, but Sugriv reminded them that the bird was only a messenger and it wouldn't be fair to hurt him. He picked him up and released him into the air in the direction of Lanka.

Rama was walking up and down on the sand, trying to solve a different kind of problem. How was the monkey army going to cross the sea? A few of them could fly, but only a very few had the magic powers. Perhaps the god of the sea would help by pushing aside the waves and clearing a dry path through the water all the way to Lanka. Rama thought that, if he prayed hard enough, the sea-god would listen to him, so he arranged a cushion of wild grass on the beach and sat down to meditate.

Three days and nights went by, but his prayers went unanswered. The monkeys ran up and down the shore, a little distance away, and watched him anxiously, chattering and wondering what would happen. On the fourth day Rama's patience came to an end. He got up, reached for his bow, played irritably with the string and said, 'I am tired of waiting for an answer. Why doesn't the sea-god want to help me? Am I not good enough for him?' He took a long arrow from his quiver, fitted it to the string and let it fly at great speed towards the depths of the ocean.

The waters started to foam and boil. Great bubbles formed on the surface, holding within them the gleam of rainbows. Then, with a tremendous explosion, the sea-god emerged from the ocean and walked in all his dripping splendour towards Rama. 'I can't overturn the laws of nature and create dry land in the middle of the ocean,' he told him, 'but I have thought carefully about your problem. The best solution is to build a bridge across to Lanka. Your monkeys are good workers and Nal is famous for his engineering skills. I will help you by calming the water and will show you the best place where you should build.'

Rama's temper subsided; the sea-god's plan looked like the best solution. Rama asked Sugriv to give orders for work to begin straight away. Nal the engineer sent some monkeys to gather enormous boulders from nearby mountains; others chopped down trees and carried them to the beach. The rocks and boulders were thrown into the water to make a firm base, and the tree trunks were lashed in place on top for the army to walk on. In a few days a long narrow causeway had taken shape, snaking its way across the sea. The time for military action had arrived.

Before setting off, Rama led Vibhishan to the water's edge, scooped up some water in his right hand and sprinkled it over his new friend. 'I anoint you king of Lanka,' he told Vibhishan. 'When Ravan is defeated, you will become king. This is my promise to you.'

It was time for the monkey army to begin their campaign against Ravan. Most of the monkeys marched over the bridge and some, who had special powers, flew in short bursts, sometimes landing for a rest. Still others swam until they were tired, then climbed on to the bridge to march with their fellow soldiers.

They were in high spirits and confident of victory. The thumping of their feet, their cheers and singing rang down to the depths of the ocean and the god of the sea sent them his blessing from below.

Ravan watched them coming from his balcony. The procession kept advancing from beyond the horizon in seemingly endless succession. On and on they came, first the monkeys then the leaders of the army, Sugriv, Hanuman, Rama, Lakshman, Jambuvan and all the others.

Even at this stage some people tried to persuade

Ravan to give up Sita to Rama, but he was in no mood to listen to anyone. His old grandfather hobbled over to talk some sense into him, but was ignored. Ravan was busy positioning his huge army to meet the coming challenge. Who could win against his numbers?

As soon as the monkey army had all arrived on the enemy's shore, Sugriv inspected his soldiers. Then it was Rama's turn to address the troops: 'The demons are masters of magic and can disguise themselves in any way they wish. Be careful how you fight, whom you attack, and victory be yours!'

No sooner had he finished speaking than Sugriv impulsively raced to Ravan's balcony and gripped his waist in a tight hold. He was keyed up and his excitement had made him quite reckless. He cried, 'Your hour has come, Ravan! We are here to destroy you!' Both Ravan and Sugriv were expert wrestlers and they threw one hold after another, trying to gain the upper hand. Ravan was beginning to tire and Sugriv noticed that he was about to use his magic powers. He knew he would have little effect against Ravan's spells. He flung Ravan's great bulk to the ground and scampered back to the safety of his own army.

Ravan's spy, Shuka, was called and asked to point out the chief warriors in the enemy ranks. From the demon king's balcony he identified Rama. 'Look, Highness, there he is; that tall, handsome prince with long, matted hair and a deerskin vest. See his mighty bow and his long feathered arrows? Next to him is Lakshman, younger but equally dignified and strong. There is Sugriv, who has just visited you; Angad, son of Bali and stepson of Sugriv; next to him Jambuvan the bear, then the mighty Hanuman – who is known to you – Nal, builder of the causeway, Nil the commander, Vinata, Kesari.' He named the chief monkeys one by one. 'There is Vibhishan, your brother, whom Rama has named king of Lanka,' Shuka said, faltering a little over this information.

Ravan turned on him with a ferocious snarl and gave him a hefty blow. 'What do I care?' he shouted. 'I am going to kill each one of them!' Then he summoned his cleverest sorcerer and ordered him to make an exact replica of Rama's head. 'It will deceive Sita into thinking that her husband is dead. Then perhaps she will marry me and Rama will have to slink back to the mainland in disgrace.'

A perfect replica of Rama's head, dripping with blood as though it had just been severed from the body, was brought on a silver plate. Holding it high and chuckling horribly, Ravan carried it to the Ashok Garden and thrust it under Sita's face. 'He has been defeated,' he said to the shocked princess. 'His spirit has long since left his body. Now will you be my wife?'

At that very moment, a servant came racing to the garden to say, 'Hurry, sire, at once! The enemy is at the city gate.'

18 The Great Battle

The throbbing of drums and the hullabaloo of battle-cries sounded in the distance. 'Hail to Rama! Hail to Lakshman! Hurrah for Sugriv and Hanuman!'

If the monkey army has advanced so far, Sita thought, then it is impossible that Rama is dead! She dried her eyes and looked up to confront her tormentor, but he had gone already. One of the ogresses, who all along had felt sorry for her, gave her comfort. 'Don't worry, Sita. Ravan has deceived you. Rama is not dead at all. Do not grieve, but start preparing to leave Lanka. The battle has begun and Ravan is sure to lose. Soon he won't have the power to keep you here any longer.'

From his balcony Ravan watched as the two armies met – an awe-inspiring sight. There was a moment of calm before the storm, then a tremendous roar erupted as they charged into combat. He saw a storm of banners, arms flailing and thrashing, arrows flying like hordes of black locusts, horses rearing and soldiers from the two sides breaching opposing ranks. Swords and maces clashing and clanging, arrows whirring and humming, animals whinnying and trumpeting, and shouts – both triumphant and despairing – filled the ears of the demon king.

'Attack from the sides!' he shouted to his generals. A fresh wave of demon soldiers descended on the monkey army, hacking and destroying but unable to gain control. There were spectacular duels between individuals: Angad and Indrajit, Hanuman and the demon generals.

Rama and Lakshman's arrows covered their friends as they fought fiercely. By nightfall the field was littered with the corpses of monkeys and demons. Indrajit and Angad were still fighting when Indrajit realized that Angad was being protected by Rama's arrows. He turned around to face Rama, took aim and fired serpent darts at him and Lakshman. They were steeped in a deadly venom which entered the princes' bloodstream and immediately sent them into a deep coma.

There was panic among the monkeys when Rama and Lakshman fell. To everyone present it looked as though they had been mortally wounded. The news travelled to Ravan, who clapped his hands with jubilation. 'Fetch Sita in the Pushpakvimaan chariot and fly her over the battlefield so she can see her dead heroes with her own eyes,' he ordered maliciously.

Poor Sita was hustled into the magic chariot, which took off and hovered over the sea of corpses. She could make out the outstretched forms of Rama and Lakshman below her. Once again she was nearly made to believe that Rama was dead, but again the kindly ogress assured her that it was an illusion. 'They are only wounded and will soon be up, fighting again. Don't be discouraged,' she said soothingly to her prisoner.

Indeed, at that very moment the great bird Garud, who was the extremely ancient father of Sampati and Jatayu, appeared on the scene and drew up the serpent darts into his own body by a magic magnetic power. As soon as the poisonous darts left their bodies, Rama and Lakshman woke up, got to their feet and were immediately in the thick of battle again. Shouts of joy rang out as the monkey army cheered their leaders, and Ravan's ten faces scowled when he heard the news.

One by one he ordered his most experienced

generals into battle. One by one they were slain by the single-minded attacks waged by the monkeys. Neel, Nal, Hanuman, Angad, Jambuvan and the other stalwart warriors fought hand-to-hand combats. When Ravan's commander-in-chief was killed by Neel, Ravan could hold himself back no longer.

'It's time I went and tackled that dwarfish human prince myself. Until Rama is dead we will have no peace,' he fumed, arming himself to the teeth and striding forward to meet his doom.

The last round was an epic battle which lasted two whole days and nights. In the initial stage Rama rode on Hanuman's shoulders and fought with Ravan until all the demon's weapons were shattered and his many golden crowns rolled on the ground, smashed to smithereens. In the evening light, the sky appeared to be stained the colour of blood and the ground was soaked in red. Bodies lay all around and darkness was falling fast. 'Get up, Ravan,' Rama said. 'Go home for the night. We will resume again tomorrow after we have both rested.'

Ravan was now beginning to feel alarmed so he sent a message to his brother Kumbhkarna for help. It took many hours to attract his attention, because Kumbhkarna loved to sleep and no one could wake him up, not even for an emergency like this. As he also loved his food, Ravan's servants made an enormous meal for him so he could feast on it as soon as he opened his eyes. Mountains of rice and meat and pitchers of fresh blood stood waiting for him. The servants blew trumpets in his ear and drove elephants to walk all over him until finally he stirred a little, gave a great yawn and got up, grumbling and rubbing his eyes. In a horrible display of gluttony he gulped down his meal and stumbled out to the battlefield with his spear held aloft. Because he was suffering from terrible indigestion his temper was high and, wielding his weapons, he mowed a path of destruction through the monkey ranks. 'Rama's blood! Lakshman's blood! Give me pints to quench my thirst!'

It took many hours and all of Rama and Lakshman's fighting skills to bring him down. After they had cut off his enormous legs, Kumbhkarna still managed to stumble around on his torso and wreak more havoc. But at last Rama pierced his neck with an arrow. With a great blow from his sword he cut off the demon's head, after which Ravan's fearful brother was no more.

Now Indrajit, Ravan's son, rushed forward with his magic weapon and aimed it at the two princes. It spun around like a glittering firework, striking them a glancing blow and knocking them out. Rama and Lakshman lay on the battlefield, unconscious for the second time, and Indrajit ran, rejoicing, with the news to his father.

The monkey army fell into disarray. Rumours flew around that Rama had been killed. 'What shall we do now? What will happen to Princess Sita?' the monkeys demanded. It took all of Hanuman's encouragement to keep the soldiers going. He ran here and there, lending his support wherever it was needed, lifting his head to shout the rallying cry, 'Victory to Rama! Victory to Lakshman! Victory to the Ikshvaku dynasty!'

Now Jambuvan trundled up to Hanuman and spoke to him urgently: 'Hurry to the Himalaya mountains. Between Mount Kailash and Rishabha is the Hill of Herbs. Quickly, gather the four herbs growing there and bring them back so that we can revive our princes.'

Hanuman sprang up to obey the old bear. He leapt into the sky, flying high in the stratosphere to get to the Himalayas as fast as possible. Very soon he had landed on the Hill of Herbs, but he couldn't identify the four herbs so he uprooted the whole hill and carried it back to the battlefield in Lanka in the palm of his hand.

The mere aroma of the herbs was so powerful that it was sufficient to revive Rama and Lakshman. They sat up groggily, rubbing their eyes, and asked

Hanuman what had happened. Very soon they were on their feet again, and the battle continued.

Now Indrajit played another nasty trick. With the aid of powerful magic spells he made a likeness of Sita and carried it aloft in Ravan's flying chariot, the Pushpakvimaan. There, in full view of Rama, he plunged a dagger into the conjured-up body. But Vibhishan, who knew about his nephew's ability to deceive, was able to assure Rama and Lakshman that the apparition was not really Sita at all.

Lakshman was so incensed by Indrajit's underhand methods that he let fly an arrow, straight and true, which sliced Indrajit's head clean off his shoulders. At this point the monkeys, sensing that their hour of triumph had nearly arrived, invaded Ravan's capital and in a frenzy of destruction swarmed all over it, burning everything they could find.

Ravan was almost maddened by the news of his son Indrajit's death. 'Was this why I brought you up, dandled you on my knees, taught you my magic spells, trained you in the art of war? Why did you have to die so young and leave me to mourn you? Oh, your poor forsaken mother, your most wretched and unlucky father!' Now Ravan was almost ready to surrender to the monkey army, but he vengefully decided to kill Sita first. Fortunately he had counsellors who had more sense than he did. 'Kill a woman?' they cried. 'Have you taken leave of your senses? Come, pull yourself together again and go out and fight. You are the demon king! Terror is on your side! This time luck too may be with you.'

All his subjects were out in the streets tearing their hair, beating their breasts and bewailing their lost homes and fortunes. The end of Lanka seemed to be in sight.

Ravan mounted his chariot for the last time and rode out once more into the fray. Brandishing his mace, baring his teeth and rolling his eyes, he presented the most terrifying spectacle ever seen. The sky seemed to lower and take on a sinister, dusky tinge; the earth seemed to growl and rumble from its bowels. Lightning played a nervous game in the heavens and thunder clapped for attention.

The first obstacle in Ravan's way was Lakshman, who let fly a shower of arrows at him. Each one of them glanced off him without making any impression on his awesome bulk. He strode on deliberately and purposefully till he was facing Rama, and then out of his mouths came a dreadful bellow of passionate hatred and rage.

He charged at his enemy, the puny human prince whom he had laughed at not long ago. Rama braced himself, holding his position, and flung his divine discus at Ravan. It spun around with the speed of the god of war himself, giving out a high-pitched whining noise which drowned out all the other sounds of the battle. There was an explosion when it met its mark. It hit Ravan in the one place which covered his invincibility, the weakest spot in his physique. As soon as the razor-sharp discus pierced his chest he uttered a cry that rang from one end of the world to the other. Crows fell from their perches on trees and fish somersaulted out of the depths of the ocean. Snakes and bats and other unlucky creatures were stunned unconscious as Ravan's bow dropped from his hand. His head jerked backwards, his twenty knees buckled slowly under him and he fell like a collapsing tower from his chariot to the place from which no one returns.

Trumpets sounded all over the battlefield and pandemonium broke out as soon as he died. The monkeys threw their weapons in the air, embraced one another and came running to touch the feet of Rama and Lakshman. By the side of Ravan's gigantic corpse, his brother Vibhishan shed a tear of regret as he remembered their childhood and the times when they had been close to each other.

19 Sita Reclaimed

There and then, on the smoking battlefield smelling of blood and death, Rama crowned Vibhishan king of Lanka. 'Hail to the new king!' rang through the air so loudly that the carrion crows flapped their black wings and flew away. Then another cry arose: 'Victory and hail to Rama, Lakshman and Sita!'

The cry reverberated over and over again and reached Sita's ears, where she was waiting anxiously in the Ashok Garden. She was completely exhausted by worry and tension. For three days her fears and hopes had alternated in quick succession. She had tried to still her mind in meditation and prayer, but doubt and anxiety had kept intruding into her thoughts. When she heard the triumphant 'Victory and hail to Rama,

Lakshman and Sita!' such relief flooded through her that she almost fainted. When she opened her eyes there was her old friend Hanuman standing in front of her, hands respectfully folded in front of his battle-scarred chest.

'I have come to fetch you, dear Princess,' he said in his gentle voice. 'But, before we leave, should I kill the demonesses who have been your prison guards for all these long months?'

'No, Hanuman, let them be. Now they will have time to reflect upon their evil ways and have a chance to change their thinking. Besides, one of them has been very good to me.' She smiled at the kindly ogress. But behind the smile Sita's heart was pounding because she could not understand why Rama had not come to fetch her himself. Surely he must be longing to see her just as much as she was longing to see him?

Hanuman read the unspoken question in her eyes. He was also very surprised to have been sent to fetch Sita. 'Prince Rama requests that you bathe and dress in fresh clothes and then accompany me to the city,' he informed her.

Sita was bewildered. 'But I would like to go with you immediately, without wasting another minute,' she protested.

'Those were my instructions,' Hanuman said quietly,

so Sita retired to wash and change her clothes before going with Hanuman to meet her husband. Rama had told Hanuman to bring Sita in a covered palanquin, which is like a sedan chair carried by four persons. As soon as the palanquin was set down, Sita alighted, her face full of joy and anticipation. Happiness and relief had brought colour into her cheeks, and her eyes shone with anticipation. She looked lovelier than ever before, her long hair now carefully combed and hanging down her back. Rama stood before her, covered in dirt and sweat, his clothes splashed with the blood of his enemies, his eyes full of the horrors of what he had seen on the battlefield. She moved towards him. 'My dear husband,' she said, her voice full of tender emotion. Tears spilled down and she started to sob uncontrollably.

Everyone looked at Rama in bewilderment, for he seemed cool and unaffected by Sita's appearance and made no sign of welcoming his long-lost wife over whom such a devastating battle had just been fought.

Sita could not at all understand his lack of emotion. She cried out brokenly, 'Whatever is the matter, my own Rama? Have you forgotten your Sita?'

Rama's reply sent shock-waves through the assembly. 'I have done my duty as a warrior. I have rescued you and defeated the forces of evil. But now, I'm afraid, our paths must separate. You have been in the home of another man for nearly a year. I will never know what really happened between you and Ravan, so I cannot take you back as my wife.'

Sita gasped and gripped the end of her garment as though it could lend her support.

Lakshman stepped forward. 'This is outrageous, brother,' he protested violently. 'How can you doubt my sister-in-law's faithfulness? She has suffered so much; why are you torturing her now, when you should be taking her in your arms and comforting her?'

In the hushed silence no one dared to breathe. Rama addressed Sita again. 'If you are as pure as you say, then you should undergo the test of fire. If you come out unharmed, it will be plain to the whole world that you are the same Sita whom I married and lived with for fifteen years.'

Sita's look of dejection turned to one of resolution. 'Test me then,' she said with quiet dignity. 'I have nothing to fear. Make a fire now and I will enter its furnace heat. The gods already know that I will endure it without blemish or mark.'

Kindling was fetched and arranged in a large heap. The fire was lit and the flames glowed orange and yellow and blue. Everyone tensed as Sita slowly walked into the fire. But as the flames caressed her, the god of fire appeared beside her. Effortlessly he picked her up, walked out of the heat and smoke and carefully set her down next to Rama.

'She is the highest in womanhood, the most matchless princess who ever lived. Serve her and love her all your life,' he proclaimed.

Then Rama turned to Sita, embraced her and held her for a long time close to himself. With a voice full of feeling and tenderness he said, 'I knew you were completely faithful and untouched by any sort of impurity. I would never have risked your life in the fire if I hadn't been completely certain of you. But I had to put you through the test so that nobody should have any reason to doubt you. Now you are with me again, I will look after you and protect you always.'

Sita's faithfulness, her quiet confidence and dignity shamed anybody who might have doubted her. Among Hindus, the highest compliment that can be said about a woman is, 'She is a Sita come to life!'

Looking as radiant as the morning sun in spring, Rama addressed the huge crowd of well-wishers and friends. 'We have been away from Ayodhya for too long. Our fourteen years of exile are now over. We will take our leave and start for home this very night.' After they had thanked everyone, Sugriv, Hanuman,

Lakshman, Rama, Sita and Vibhishan mounted the magic chariot Pushpakvimaan and started on their journey back to Kishkindha and then to Ayodhya.

20 The End of the Exile

*A*s the chariot winged its way over sea and land, Rama and Hanuman pointed out sights and landmarks to Sita. 'There is the great causeway built by Nal. Can you see? Just there, to the right, is the shore from which we started. Look, the hill on which Hanuman meditated!' They traced the forest paths which had led from Kishkindha to the sea until at last they saw the capital of Sugriv's kingdom beneath them. 'Shall we pick up your wife on our way to Ayodhya? You are all invited to my coronation,' Rama said to the monkey king.

It was a long journey, even in the magic flying chariot. Hanuman had disembarked in Kishkindha to make room for Sugriv's wife. He flew ahead on his own to alert Bharat and Vashishta that Rama was on the way and that preparations for the coronation ceremony should begin.

He found Bharat wan and haggard, aged beyond his years, weighed down by the responsibilities of governing Koshal. He was counting the days to Rama's return. Kausalya and Sumitra were beside themselves with joy at the prospect of Rama, Sita and Lakshman's return and they joyfully started to arrange their welcome. Even Kaikeyi was relieved that they were safe and sound. Sumantra began to polish Rama's chariot and groom the horses, and all the palace retainers bustled about in a frenzy of excitement. The court jester polished his act; the head gardener stood over the under-gardeners, pointing out every little weedling; the royal garland maker threaded marigolds and jasmine and roses to make extravagant necklaces of fresh flowers; and the cooks excelled themselves with the number and variety of delicacies which they created in the kitchens.

The townspeople were ready with perfumed water and baskets of flower-petals when the Pushpakvimaan touched down. The royal trio stepped out, followed by their faithful friends. Bharat looked long at Rama's face for signs of any change. Of course he was older, but, besides the nobility and wisdom and kindness, Bharat detected a glow of inner fulfilment and peace.

He bent down, slipped Rama's old, worn sandals off his feet, then eased his feet into the unworn pair that had been symbols of his kinghood since Rama had been away.

Rama, Lakshman and Sita met everyone with the greatest joy and warmth. They touched the feet of their elders and embraced everyone else. Then they drank in the air of their beloved Ayodhya and rested their eyes on the familiar landmarks. It was good to be home again.

Sita was escorted by the mothers to her apartments in the palace and relieved of her coarse clothing. Kausalya had arranged for her to be bathed in warm water, perfumed with rose essence. Then she was massaged with sandalwood oil and her long hair was carefully dressed and decorated with flowers. Lovingly her maids robed her in the softest silk and draped necklaces of precious stones round her neck. Golden earrings were put in her ears, together with golden bracelets and anklets on her arms and feet. The simple, dusty, weary hermit's wife was transformed into the most enchantingly beautiful princess, who was soon to be crowned consort to Rama's king.

The coronation took place with magnificent splendour. The gods witnessed the ceremonies from heaven and prophesied that a reign of righteous government would now begin. Because there was order in the kingdom, everyone would benefit from it. People would be happier than they had ever been before; learning and the arts would flourish and everyone's behaviour would be guided by decency and virtue.

Rama spent long hours in conference with Vibhishan and Sugriv. He gave them good advice about ruling their kingdoms and promised them eternal friendship.

All too soon it was time for the gallant Hanuman to leave too. 'We will always be together in spirit, you and I, Lakshman and Sita,' Rama said, embracing the extraordinary monkey. He prophesied, 'Whenever people talk about us, they will talk about you, for we are inseparable.'

Sita wanted to give Hanuman something special for himself. She unclasped the heavy rope of finest sea-pearls from her neck and placed it round Hanuman's. 'I will never be able to thank you enough for all you have done for us, but my prayers will always be with you,' she told him. Hanuman bowed to her, folded his hands in farewell, lifted himself upwards and flew back to Kishkindha.

To this day, Hanuman's name is always linked with those of Rama and Sita. As long as their story is told in the world, his name will be honoured with theirs. It is said that when Rama's name is even whispered, Hanuman's presence is felt. Along with Rama and Sita, the valiant and gentle monkey is part of the Hindu gods and divine beings.

Glossary of names and Indian words

Angad son of Bali
ashok a species of tree
ashram a holy place
Ayodhya capital of Koshal
Bali a monkey – brother of Sugriv
Bharat son of Dasharath and Kaikeyi
Brahma a Hindu god (the Creator)
Chitrakoot a hill
Dandak a forest
Dasehra a festival in October
Dasharath king of Koshal; father of Rama
Diwali the festival of lights, following Dasehra
Ganga a holy river (often called Ganges)
Garud father of Jatayu and Sampati
Godavari a river
Hanuman the monkey god; son of the wind god
Ikshvaku dynasty to which Dasharath and Rama belong
Indrajit son of Ravan
Jambuvan a bear
Janak king of Mithila; father of Sita
Jatayu a divine bird; brother of Sampati
Kaikeyi youngest wife of Dasharath; mother of Bharat
Kailash a mountain in the Himalayas
Kausalya eldest wife of Dasharath; mother of Rama
Kesari a monkey
Khara younger brother of Ravan
Kishkindha capital of the monkey kingdom
Koshal land ruled by King Dasharath
Krishna a Hindu god
Kumbhkarna brother of Ravan
Lakshman twin son of Dasharath and Sumitra
Lanka kingdom ruled by Ravan
Manthara woman-in-waiting to Kaikeyi
Mareech a demon

Mithila city ruled by King Janak

Nal a monkey engineer

Neel a monkey

Nil a commander of the monkey army

Pampa a river

Panas a monkey

Panchavati a region by the River Godavari

Pushpakvimaan Ravan's flying chariot

rakshasas demons

Rama eldest son of Dasharath and Kausalya

Ramlila re-enactment of the *Ramayana*

Ramrajya Rama's rule; the ideal kingdom

Ravan king of the demons

Rishabha a mountain in the Himalayas

rishis holy men

Rishyamukh a hill

Sampati a divine bird; son of the dawn god

Sanskrit language of ancient Indian scriptures and literature

Sarayu a river

Saroopanakha sister of Ravan

Shatrughan twin brother of Lakshman

Shiva a Hindu god

Shuka a demon

Sita bride of Rama

Subahu a demon

Sugriv a monkey – brother of Bali

Sumantra Dasharath's charioteer

Sumitra middle wife of Dasharath; mother of Lakshman and Shatrughan

Surayu river separating Ayodhya from the wilderness

Tataka ogress – mother of Mareech

tilak mark a mark made on the forehead with sandalwood paste

Varun wind god

Vashishta Dasharath's chief adviser

Vibhishan younger brother of Ravan

Vinata a monkey

Vishnu a Hindu god

Vishwamitra hermit and sage